Dolly caught Matt's eye. 'Does that mean you're willing to let us have the farmhouse?' she asked Turner, keeping her voice from trembling.

Turner hesitated a moment before replying. 'I have no objection, though the final decision must be with the company. It has occurred to me though, Matt, Jesse retires in ten months or so. If you were willing to take his place you could have the house rent free – completely modernized. Think it over. You'd have a free house, a first class wage, and you'd be more or less your own boss, with the money to buy the finest sheep and build the best flock in the country!'

Matt and Dolly stared at each other in bewilderment.

Very slowly Matt said, 'I've never even thought on it . . . not afore tonight.'

LEE MACKENZIE

Family Feuds
Emmerdale Farm Book 19

Based on the successful
❧ Yorkshire Television series
originated by Kevin Laffan

FONTANA PAPERBACKS

First published by Fontana Paperbacks 1984

Copyright © Lee Mackenzie 1984
Front cover photograph © Yorkshire Television Ltd
Emmerdale and Emmerdale Farm
are Trade Marks of Yorkshire Television Ltd

Made and printed in Great Britain by
William Collins Sons & Co Ltd, Glasgow

Chapter One

Just before Jack Sugden made his sudden announcement that he and Pat Merrick were going to get wed in three weeks' time, Dolly Skilbeck told a secret to her husband. It was a happy secret, one that Matt was glad to hear.

Dolly was pregnant again.

She dearly wanted a baby. She felt that time was slipping by and they had no family of their own, only the family at Emmerdale who had more or less adopted them and whom they loved. Yes, they loved Annie and Sam – but it wasn't the same as having children, something of your very own to care for, something or rather someone who would carry on Matt's name.

Dolly had been pregnant before, but had lost the baby. Matt was anxious for her now, because after that last occasion Dolly had gone into a post-natal depression which had really scared him.

'There's nowt to worry about, Matt. Honestly,' Dolly soothed. 'Doctor says I'm fine. And this time I'll be ever so careful, and –'

'You were careful last time, love,' he said. 'It had nowt to do with anything you did. Doctor said. So this time you've got to do even less –'

'Now that's logic!' She was laughing. Then she laid her fair head against his and snuggled against him. 'It's going to be fine this time,' she said. 'I know it is. Something tells me.'

This blissful state lasted a day or two. They hugged the secret to themselves, so that it kept them a little apart from all the troubles that poor Jack was going through. There was a dreadful uproar about a helicopter, hired by N.Y. Estates to do some crop-spraying, which overflew Emmerdale land panicking the pedigree Friesians into a mini-stampede. The result was the death of one cow and injury to two others. Jack was furious with N.Y. Estates but there was nothing unusual about that – Jack was apt to get angry with them at the slightest cause.

This time, however, he had good reason. He refused to take a cheque from his brother Joe when Joe, trying to smooth matters over, offered it in compensation. 'N.Y.'s pilot is to blame and N.Y. are going to pay,' insisted Jack. And before too long they did so, anxious not to have bad publicity over the affair.

Dolly could see Matt was involved in this row, but she herself somehow couldn't take it too seriously. It was only Jack getting in a state about his principles again. Dolly was more interested in thinking about the coming of the baby, and what life would be like once he had arrived. He – she was sure it would be a boy . . .

'You know, Matt, it's going to be a terrible squeeze at Emmerdale once he's here,' she pointed out.

'Gerron wi' thee!' Matt teased. 'He'll only be a little chap!'

'No, seriously – listen, Matt. Of course he'll share our room for a bit, but then he'll need a room of his own –'

'Happen. But that's a year ahead –'

'But Matt . . . Suppose Jack and Pat Merrick really do get married?'

'Nay,' said Matt. 'The way things are at t'moment, they're further apart than they ever were.'

It appeared to be true – then. Jack and Pat had scarcely exchanged a word for weeks. No one knew the ins and outs of it. Jack had announced to his mother that he and Pat were going to get married, then estrangement seemed to set in. It had something to do with the way Jack handled Pat's son, Jackie – or rather mishandled him. It had become common knowledge that Jackie was in fact not the son of Pat's legal husband Tom Merrick, but the son of Jack Sugden, conceived before Pat ever married Tom.

Jack had mistakenly imagined that this would form some sort of bond between him and Jackie, but just the opposite happened: Jackie couldn't stand Jack.

Naturally strains ensued. Somehow the idea of the marriage between Jack and Pat had receded. So Matt, who tended to take things as they came, didn't worry about that. He felt they could fit Dolly's baby quite happily into the household at Emmerdale as it then existed.

He overlooked one point: the nestbuilding instincts of a

pregnant woman. Dolly longed for a house of her own. She and Matt had gone to look at more than one property in the neighbourhood since she first started murmuring that it would be nice to have a place they could call home, but always the obstacles were too great. Either the cottage was too far from Emmerdale for Matt to get there easily for milking, or else the price was beyond them.

Generally it was the latter. Houses and cottages in the Dales were snapped up as holiday homes, for sums that were beyond the purse of the local inhabitants. Dolly and Matt had no funds except their own savings and the share of Emmerdale Farm Limited that belonged to Matt – and naturally he wouldn't sell that. He might have raised a loan for a mortgage on it, but the mortgage repayments would have crippled them.

Matt didn't get a big wage from Emmerdale, never had and didn't expect it. In fact, they only lived as comfortably as they did because they shared the accommodation and catering at the farm. If they moved to a house a fair distance away, he would have to run a car, and they would have to pay their own housekeeping, including heating and lighting and rates and all the rest . . . Dolly knew the figures inside out. She had been doing sums on pieces of paper ever since she discovered that the baby was coming.

But, as the ancient saying goes, where there's a will there's a way. One evening, as they were coming home from a stroll, they paused to lean on the old stone wall at the lower edge of the area which contained Emmerdale's outbuildings. The May sun shone on the landscape, gilding the roofs with subdued gold. The trees were almost in full leaf. The old chestnut to the south of the barn was beginning to show its candles.

'Eeh,' breathed Matt, 'when you look around you evenings like this, you can't help feeling the world's a good place for all its drawbacks.'

'Aye, lad,' Dolly agreed.

He put an arm around her. 'Still feeling all right?'

'Fine, Matt, fine . . . Only thing is, I'd still feel happier if we could just get a place of our own.'

'I know, lass, but we've tried everything . . .'

'Other farms provide cottages for their workers, you

know, Matt. I think you should put it up to Jack and the others that you would like accommodation –'

'But I've got accommodation, Dolly. Always have had. A nice comfy room –'

'That's not really good enough though, is it? We've got to think of the future. We don't want our baby growing up without enough room to breathe –'

Matt laughed and jerked his head towards the view. 'Now that won't work, Dolly! Look round you – there's room enough for the whole population of Beckindale to breathe on Emmerdale land. Though mind you, we might have to pack 'em into the mistle and the sheds if it came on to rain.'

Dolly allowed herself to relent and giggled a little. But his words struck a chord. She stared at the farm buildings. 'Matt . . .'

'Aye?'

'What about the barn?'

'What about it?'

'It's only used for storing big machinery and feed, after all . . .'

'So it is. I never knew you were interested in what's stored where.'

'No, listen, love, I'm serious. That barn's a good size.'

'A good size for what?'

'A home, Matt!'

Matt gave a roar of laughter. 'What, live in a barn? I've heard some daft remarks in my time . . . ! Folk say when you leave a door open behind you, "What's the matter with you, were you brought up in a barn?", but –'

'Nay, don't laugh,' Dolly said, pummelling him in the chest with her fists. 'I'm serious. That barn could be converted into a right comfortable little house.'

Matt examined her face, and saw that she really meant it. He frowned, then turned to look at the barn. It was a capacious building, roomy and high, with an area about the same as the ground floor of Emmerdale's kitchen and parlour. He began to think of it as the interior of a house. You could have a little sitting-room and a biggish kitchen, and over those you could put in a couple of bedrooms and a bathroom . . .

It was in fact possible. The stonework was solid, the walls about a foot thick. But though that meant protection against the wild winds of the Dales in winter and coolness in summer, it also meant terrible problems in making alterations.

'It would be a big job, love,' he said in a tone of doubt. 'You'd have to put in drainage, and electricity –'

'It's got electricity – there's overhead light in it, I've seen you working in there in winter –'

'Aye, but I mean you'd have to put in power for things like washing machines . . . And laying drains is a terrible business.'

'We could get a builder in to do the difficult bits,' she urged. 'But you're so good with your hands, Matt – you could do most of the stonework and woodwork and painting –'

'That roof would need renovating.'

'Happen we could have it heightened – give more room for the upper floor –'

'Hey-up!' he said suddenly. 'You're talking big money, you know, Dolly. You couldn't make that place fit to live in for just a penny piece. It'd need a big investment.'

'But it'd be a lot less than trying to buy a completed house or cottage hereabouts, Matt. And it would solve all the problems about being near your work.' She chuckled, pleased with what she was going to say. 'You'd be on top of your work here!'

He couldn't help but be attracted by the idea. The old barn was solid and reliable. Since it belonged to Emmerdale Farm, they wouldn't be expected to buy it before renovating. Once it was converted into a home, they wouldn't have to pay rent. The only outlay would be the cost of the conversion and though that wouldn't be small, Matt felt they had enough resources to meet the cost.

'Let's go and take a look inside,' Dolly suggested, taking his hand. They went through the gate in the stone wall, into the farm's outer yard, and came to the great wooden door of the barn. Matt swung open one side. Within was a deep, echoing darkness. He felt for the switch at the right hand side of the entrance. A light came on overhead, only just sufficient to reach to the corners of the old building. The shapes of the big old harrow and the sprayer came into view. There were some plastic sacks of feed stacked neatly in the far forner. Other than that, the place was almost empty – there was plenty of room for them to walk down the barn and survey it from the other end.

'It could be nice, Matt!' Dolly exclaimed in excitement. 'It's bigger inside than I thought.'

'That's always deceptive. And once you start putting up partition walls . . .'

'But it could work, Matt! It could make a lovely little home.'

He was silent. His round face was thoughtful. What his wife suggested was possible but all the same it was a big undertaking. It was going to cost not hundreds but thousands, and though they had a bit put by, it would soon dwindle once they began investing it in a building job as big as this. 'Let's consider it for a bit,' he said at last. 'It wants thinking on, love. I mean, we don't want to start talking about it and getting estimates and all that, and then find we go off the idea in a week or two.'

'I won't go off the idea, Matt. I really think it's the solution to all our problems.'

She might be right, at that. But Matt Skilbeck was never one to leap into sudden action. He liked to take his time. 'Well, if it's such a good idea we'll still think so in ten days' time. So let's sleep on it, Dolly – let's leave it to simmer until we really feel convinced about it.'

'Until *you're* convinced,' she said with a gurgle of laughter.

'All right, until *I'm* convinced. I don't want to start any more discussions and arguments until we have to. Annie's just about had enough, what with Jack and his problems and the thing about the helicopter.'

'All right, love,' Dolly said in a tone of mischief. 'I'll be good.'

But he could see her mind was made up. She'd seen a way to get a home of her own, and she intended to stick to it. And why not? She had a right to it, after all. And she was keen on the idea. She'd go out on some pretext and there she'd be, surveying the barn with a proprietorial eye.

Then came Jack's amazingly sudden announcement.

10

The marriage with Pat Merrick was on again. Not only on, but imminent. He'd taken out a licence and they'd be wed in three weeks' time. 'You see?' Dolly said to Matt. 'Good thing we've got our own plans made. What on earth would it be like with you and me and Annie and Grandad and Jack and Pat and Jackie and Sandie all living in the same house? We'd be bursting out at the seams.'

He had to admit she was right, and had been right to be thinking ahead. 'Oh, I'm not just a pretty face,' she laughed when he complimented her on her wisdom. 'Will you tell them what we have in mind at the farm meeting tonight?'

'Aye, best to get it sorted. I wish I'd had time to get some estimates of the cost, though.'

'That doesn't matter for the moment, love. Thing is, to show them we've got a good grip on the idea, that it's not just a passing fancy.' She paused and gave his arm a loving squeeze. 'You were right, you see, about giving it time to simmer. We can say we thought it all through for a week or so and we still think it would work as a house for us.'

'Aye,' agreed Matt. He seemed a little preoccupied. 'I wonder what the farm meeting's about . . . ?'

'Oh, Jack's wedding plans, I s'pose –'

'Nay, that's not company business. Jack'd chat about that wi' Annie on a personal basis. No, I suppose Jack's got some new idea about t'farm he wants to put up to us.'

'What'll it be this time?' Dolly wondered. 'Buying traditional milk-cows instead of Friesians? Bee-keeping?'

He tried to look disapproving with her but it didn't quite work. The fact was, there was no knowing what daft idea Jack had got in his head. Organic farming only on one section of Emmerdale land, stubborn opposition to almost anything that N.Y. Estates decided to do, objections to the moving of footpaths – you name it, Jack was into it. 'Well, we'll know in a minute,' he murmured. 'Best get downstairs to it.'

They were in their big upstairs room at the farmhouse. The farm meeting would take place in the kitchen. While it went on, Dolly and Sam Pearson would be banished to the parlour, because they were not shareholders in the farm. 'Don't thee be too long about it, love,' Dolly warned

11

him in playful tones. 'You know I'm bursting to know what happens when they hear our plans for the barn.'

'Don't worry, it'll go like a newly greased tractor,' Matt prophesied.

He couldn't have been more wrong. The gathering in the farm kitchen was not to approve or disapprove Jack's latest notions about how to run Emmerdale. Glancing round, Matt could see that both Jack's brother and Henry Wilks, the business manager, were as much in the dark as he himself. They looked attentively at Jack, who was sitting to Annie's right. Annie, as ever, was composed but not particularly concerned. She left the running of the farm to the menfolk – it was the house which was her domain.

'Meeting of Emmerdale Farm Limited called to order,' Henry said in a businesslike tone. 'We have no other business this evening except summat that Jack wants to raise, since as a matter of fact we presented the annual report last month and the auditors are perfectly happy with the accounts. So I call on Jack to tell us what's on his mind.'

'Right,' Jack said briskly. 'It's a nice June evening so I won't hang about keeping us indoors. All I want to propose is to do with accommodation for the kids and Pat and me once we're wed. If you think about it, you'll agree that we'd be a bit pushed to give enough space to our new family in the house as it stands.'

Ah, thought Matt, he's going to suggest an extension to the farmhouse. Not a bad idea. Then, though he reproved himself for the selfishness, he thought: wonder if they'll have money for converting the barn too, if they vote money for a house extension?

'Couple of days ago,' Jack went on, 'I had a good look at the big barn, and it seemed to me it would convert into a snug little house for Pat and me.'

Matt gave a gasp. Heads turned towards him. Jack cast him a puzzled glance then went on: 'It might be a bit of a push getting three bedrooms into it –'

'Three bedrooms?' Matt echoed, helpless in the face of Jack's crisp exposition of his plan.

'Aye, one for me and Pat, and one each for Jackie and Sandie. We'd have to keep them on the small side, but Rickert says it can be done.'

'Rickert?'

'Aye, in Hotten. I took him to have a look yesterday – not a proper survey, you understand, just to give him an idea and he said he thought it could be done.'

'Cost a bit, though, won't it?' Joe enquired, tilting back his dark head to survey the cornice of the old farm kitchen. He was looking at the thickness of the wall where window met ceiling. The barn was built on the same scale – walls of stone at least a foot thick. Although Yorkshire builders are accustomed to dealing with stone, it would still be a formidable task to inset windows and doors in the walls of the barn.

'Rickert's getting out an estimate, just a rough one to give us some idea. I thought of approaching Playdon, too, and mebbe Wiles – they're well spoken of in the building trade. Then we can compare the costs and see which one to choose.'

'That's if we decide to go on with it,' Henry reminded them.

'You haven't anything against it, Henry, have you?' asked Jack.

'Not in principle. It's a right good idea, in fact. Even if the cost's a bit steep, I think we ought to go on with it. Accommodation here at Emmerdale is a bit of a problem and looks like going on that way for a good while, unless we deal with it.' He didn't explain the thought behind this, which was that Jack and Pat might have other children. Pat, after all, was still in her thirties; not by any means past childbearing, if she and Jack wanted a baby.

'Hold on a minute,' Matt said, finding his voice at last. 'About the barn –'

'You're going to say we need it,' Jack interrupted, with a little grin of amusement. 'We sometimes put ailing sheep and lambs in there in wet weather – yes, yes, I know, we'll have to get some substitute cover. But in fact, if you go and take a good look inside, you'll see that for eleven out of the twelve months it houses spare machinery and some stocks of feed or seed. There's a better use for a good building like that. We can put up something somewhere else to compensate, or if we reorganize we can probably get most of the stuff in the dutch barn or the old shed.'

13

'I took a good look,' Matt said, hearing his own words come out flat and stilted. 'About ten days ago. Me and Dolly – we looked at the old barn and we decided it would make a nice little home for the pair of us.'

'What?'

'You know Dolly's wanted a place of her own for a long time now,' he went on, staring hard at the sheet of paper which Annie always put by every place before a board meeting, in case any notes needed to be taken. 'We've looked at cottages –'

'Of course, Matt,' Annie said, with quick sympathy. Though she would have hated to part with Dolly, she well understood the girl's need to have her own home. 'I only wish you'd found something to suit. But in this case, even though you've been looking at the barn –'

'I didn't know you'd had the same idea, Matt,' Jack said. 'You never said.'

'Nay, I wanted us to be sure we really liked the notion. And it were Dolly's idea, really – a week ago last Tuesday, when we were out for a walk, she suddenly saw the barn as a little house. We went inside and made a sort of measure-up and we thought . . . we felt . . .'

'Well, it's a bit of a facer,' Jack said. 'You might have mentioned it.'

'How was I to know you were even considering the barn? In fact, you weren't,' Matt said. 'Not until a couple of days ago.'

A dreadful pause ensued. Henry Wilks cleared his throat. Joe avoided everyone else's glance. Annie had coloured a little with distress. She looked helplessly at Henry.

'Aye . . . well . . . It seems to me,' said Henry, 'that we have to go on need rather than wishes. Much though I'd like you and Dolly to have a place of your own, you've got to admit, Matt, that it makes more sense to adapt the barn to take Pat and Jack and Pat's two youngsters, rather than just you and Dolly.'

'It's not just me and Dolly,' Matt said. 'Dolly's expecting.'

The silence that followed this was worse than the first one. Matt could hear Joe draw in his breath in dismay.

Henry looked so taken aback he couldn't speak. Annie was shaking her head in concern because, although she had been let into Dolly's secret, she was suddenly being made to see its importance in this issue.

Jack at last found words to utter. 'Well, congratulations on the baby, Matt,' he said. It sounded idiotic – lame and almost insincere. A faint feeling of annoyance stirred in him. Somehow he was being made to seem in the wrong. But that wasn't the case. He had had this idea himself, just as Matt had. And it wasn't his fault that he came out with it first.

The others who were hearing the news for the first time echoed his congratulations. Matt nodded but didn't smile. He had never felt so much at a loss in his life. Just when he thought he was going to give Dolly one of the things she wanted most in the world, it looked as if it was going to be snatched away from him.

'Dolly's right keen on this idea,' he said. 'She's been trotting out to look at it every day ever since she thought of it. I can't tell her she's . . . I mean, she's not only not going to get it, somebody else is getting it.'

'It's a shame,' muttered Joe. His brother cast him a sharp glance. 'Well, it is,' he insisted.

'I'm as sorry as anybody,' Jack said. 'But what Henry said still stands. It's better sense to use the barn for four than for two people and a baby that hasn't even arrived yet. I have to think of Pat. She's had a terrible time, what with the way Tom behaved over the divorce, and making do in that pokey little caravan –'

'Hey!' said Joe. 'You were pleased enough when N.Y. Estates made it available to her –'

Jack had the grace to look momentarily shamed. He'd quite forgotten that his brother had persuaded his boss Alan Turner to hand over the caravan – which strictly speaking was for itinerant workers doing such jobs as drain-laying – to the Merricks. Pat might have come to hate the confinement of the tiny van, but she'd been thankful when it was first offered as an alternative to living with a very strict aunt. And, Jack had to admit to himself, the rent asked by N.Y. was almost a peppercorn.

'But the fact remains,' Annie intervened, 'that once she

and Jack are wed, she won't be living there any more. I'm sure Pat's grateful, Joe, and so are we when we think that you came to her rescue when she needed it. Things are different now. Our problem is how to fit Pat and her children into Emmerdale after the wedding. And Jack's idea of the barn is a good one –'

'It were Dolly's idea!' Matt insisted.

'Aye, lad,' sighed Henry. 'Trouble is, good ideas sometimes seem to be in the air – more than one person can get 'em when the time seems right. And we have to agree that Jack came out with it first.'

'Hang it,' Matt said, 'I made Dolly wait before talking about it because I didn't want to make one more problem in the middle of all the things Annie has to cope with, what with the wedding so near an' all –'

'I'm sorry, Matt,' Henry said with obvious regret, running a hand over his thinning hair. 'I don't see really what difference it makes who had the idea first. The real factor is, who needs the barn most?'

At that psychological moment, Dolly put her head round the kitchen door. She cleared her throat. 'Er . . . Can I just . . . ? Grandad wants another cup and the pot's empty.'

Everybody froze into embarrassment. Annie took a big breath and said, 'Help yourself, lass.' Dolly crossed to the Aga and filled the hot water jug from the big kettle. She could feel the atmosphere at the table behind her like a wall of cool fog. She stole a glance over her shoulder at Matt, but Matt was looking straight down at the blank sheet of paper. Dolly went back to the door with her jug of boiling water.

'Ah well,' she said to herself with feeling as she left the room, 'happy days!'

The coolness she had sensed really puzzled her. Surely they weren't going to say no to her idea? What grounds could they have? The barn was really not much used, to convert it would certainly make it an asset, and it would be the ideal solution for her and Matt. Could they be grudging the money? If they were, she thought, I'll never forgive them, after all Matt's done for this family!

After the door closed on her, everyone relaxed a little. Matt shook his head to himself. Dolly would never believe

16

what was going on, he felt . . .

'Happen the fairest way,' said Annie, 'is to toss a coin. No one could complain of being shown favour or not, then.'

Matt looked reluctant to trust the fate of Dolly's hopes to the toss of a coin. But before he could speak, Jack jumped in.

'It's nowt to do with favour, Ma. The plain fact is that there is no room here for three extra bodies. You'd be hard put to it to get 'em round the table, never mind sleeping here.'

'We'd manage,' Annie said with a confidence no one could take seriously. 'We've done it before, we could again.'

'Manage isn't good enough,' said Jack.

Matt looked up and met his eyes. Manage . . . he and Dolly had been managing in the attic bedsit ever since they got wed. It was a pleasant room, no one denied that. But it was a long way from the privacy of even the caravan belonging to N.Y. Estates.

Jack looked away and went on doggedly: 'Pat and her kids will be living here, not billeted for a couple of weeks–'

'I'd always had the idea Jackie wouldn't be living with Pat and you once you were married?' Henry intervened.

'Oh, that's just his mood at the moment. Pat wants him to. She doesn't want our marriage to break up her family, and Jackie's sure to come round.'

That's what you think, mate, Joe thought to himself. He, as Jackie's employer, saw far more of young Jackie than Jack did. He knew what Jack apparently did not, that the lad really disliked his natural father. Jack seemed to go on the old saying that blood is thicker than water, imagining it meant affection had something to do with thickness. In this case, the opposite was true. Jackie might one day have come to like Jack if only they had not been discovered to be father and son. Jackie still loved Tom Merrick as his father and resented Jack for ousting Tom from his place in the Merrick family. Joe Sugden felt it was quite a natural reaction and only wished his high-minded brother could see this simple truth.

Wilks expressed what Joe dare not. 'Pat may want Jackie

17

to come here but he's shown himself to have a will of his own. I don't know whether you can take it for granted he'll give in.' What he meant was, that would be one less to fit into Emmerdale farmhouse.

'The opportunity's got to be there,' Jack insisted. His long dark face was clenched with determination. He'd had this great idea about the barn as a home for himself and Pat's children, saw it as a solution to all their problems – which would be great enough in all conscience without being crammed into the old house. He couldn't let the barn go, not even to Matt.

'That's a fairly generous way of looking at it when we're not in a position to be quite as lordly as all that,' Joe said.

Henry frowned at him. Words like 'lordly' weren't going to help matters. 'We're just trying to solve this problem on a human footing,' he told him.

'All right, let's put it on a human footing,' said Joe, sitting up straight and looking straight at Jack. 'We're talking about using the accommodation we have and what we might create. Seems to me everyone's got to be inconvenienced except Jack!'

Jack bridled. 'What's the good of pretending summat will work out when it's plain as a pikestaff it'd only lead to trouble?'

'*Lead* to trouble? We're in trouble now!' Joe turned a sympathetic glance on Matt.

'Hardly trouble –' soothed Henry.

'I'd like to know your word for it then! We're faced with handing over the barn to Jack and doing down Matt, or giving it to Matt and making Jack miserable –'

'Don't talk about it as if it were a lollipop you were handing to a baby!' Jack said in anger.

'We'll talk about it as if we had some manners!' Annie said sharply. 'I'd like some civility from the pair of you!'

Joe raised his eyes to heaven and sat back, feeling himself the loser once again in yet another passage of arms with his brother. Henry looked at Matt. 'I think it's time we had a word from you, Matt.'

Matt took a long moment before he spoke. There was a frown of concentration between his brows. While the other two had been bickering, he'd been thinking deeply. His

18

innate respect for the Sugden family made him look at the matter from a slightly different angle.

'I can't really see as there's much I can say, after all,' he said. 'Jack's the heir, in a way. I mean, Emmerdale's more his than anyone's –'

'This is a limited company,' Joe reminded him in a sharp tone.

'That's nowt but a name and a convenience, Joe. Emmerdale Farm is the Sugdens', and, as the eldest son, Jack's got more right here than anyone –'

'I'm not trying to pull rank on you, Matt!' Jack cried, genuinely taken aback. 'I don't want –'

'There's no way you can't pull rank, Jack,' Matt said, quite collected and yet with a little edge under his manner. 'You are who you are, same as I am who I am, and neither of us is to blame for that. But it gives you first choice of the barn, I reckon. It belongs to you – how can I say you haven't the right to it? It's just that Dolly . . .'

'You know,' Jack suggested, clutching at faint hope, 'the baby's not due for a while yet, after all. You might find summat.'

'I reckon we'll just have to keep looking.' He sighed. 'Is there any other business?'

Henry shook his head with a regret he didn't know how to voice. 'Nowt as can't wait.'

'Then I'll be away. I've a couple of ewes to look at afore I take Dolly out for a drink.' A celebration drink, it was to have been. On his way to the door he paused. 'You know, there's no way that barn can be made fit to live in afore the wedding. We're going to be a bit crammed in here until it's ready, so I reckon you'd better have a think about that.'

When the door had closed on him, Jack threw down the pencil he'd been playing with. 'How is it he manages to make me feel a heel?' he cried.

Joe opened his mouth. 'Joe!' exclaimed Annie.

Joe grinned. 'I was only going to ask if there was a drink – not tea or coffee. I feel I need summat, after that!'

Annie nodded at the old-fashioned sideboard which held the supply of drink, such as it was. Jack went on in an irritated tone: 'Can I make one thing quite clear? I had no idea Matt and Dolly had their eye on the barn –'

'If you had, would you have put in your claim?' Joe asked from the sideboard.

'Of course not! I would never have broached the subject.'

'And how'd you have solved the problem of accommodation for your new family?'

'That's not the point! The point is, I did mention it first –'

'Nobody's questioning that, lad,' said his mother.

'Not out loud! But I get the feeling you all think I'm stealing a march on Matt or something – that I'm not doing right by him . . .'

'Happen that's just conscience,' murmured Joe.

'About what? What have I done wrong?'

'Who said you had?'

'You're implying –'

'No I'm not.' Joe came to the table with a can of beer and a glass. He sat down, put the glass and the can on the table, and studied them as if they were important. 'It's just . . . I reckon we all know Matt always seems to come out at the worst end of any deal that's going.'

'That's not true, Joe,' Annie protested. 'And Matt doesn't think so, either.'

'Happen,' said Joe. He began to pour the frothy lager into the glass. 'But what about Dolly?'

What about Dolly? That was the question Matt was asking himself as he walked briskly to the lambing shelter to examine the new mothers and their offspring. What about Dolly? How was he going to tell her what had happened to her happy dream?

Chapter Two

Dolly's reaction to the news was utter disbelief. 'You mean he snatched our idea for himself?' she cried.

'Nay, lass, he spoke up about it afore ever I got the chance to. He'd had the same idea.'

'Oh, Matt, I don't believe that! It's impossible. He must

20

have seen me going out to look at it – '

'Dolly, he just thought of it for himself,' Matt sighed. 'Don't go blaming him for summat he didn't do. Whatever Jack is, he's not a twister.'

They were sitting on a knoll at the far side of the twenty acre field. It was about half past seven of a fine evening in early June, with the birds of the Dales singing even now to mark their territories after a somewhat late spring. The sun was still strong in the sky. The scent of hay was in the air from the machines throbbing somewhere on N.Y.'s fields.

Matt and Dolly hadn't as yet gone to the Woolpack for the drink Matt had promised Dolly. When he told her he had bad news, to pretend they had anything to celebrate was ridiculous.

Matt tried to recall all that had been said at the meeting to recount to Dolly. She listened in growing despondency.

'I can't see why he couldn't make a sacrifice for once, Matt. It'd be a change if he put himself out for your comfort.'

Matt was uneasy at her opinion. He didn't want to criticize Jack. 'It's not a little thing like doing a good turn, love. Setting up a home's different.'

'And I suppose it doesn't matter about *us* setting up a home?'

'Of course it matters . . .' He felt helpless in face of her disappointment. 'See, Dolly, you've got to think on the basic facts. Jack is head of Sugdens – '

'Huh!' said Dolly. 'Tell that to Joe! You can see Joe thinks he makes all kinds of mistakes – '

'I'm not talking about just the farm. Jack's the eldest son. He'll inherit the house and the farm – '

'No he won't! He'll only get it if Emmerdale Farm Limited says he can! He's just a shareholder in Emmerdale Farm, that's all!'

'And farm manager – '

'Aye, and a right hash he makes of it half the time!'

'Dolly, you don't have to tell me Jack's got a lot to learn about farming. I'm the one as has to sort out the mistakes. But say what you like, Emmerdale Farm is really going to go to Jack in the end – '

'I don't see that,' Dolly said in a stubborn tone. 'You

have a share, Joe has a share, Annie has a share –'

'But you're forgetting, love . . . It were Jack as gave us the shares in the first place.'

She was silent. That had all happened before Dolly came to Beckindale, so she only knew of it through gossip. As she had heard it, Jack had come back from the funeral of his father Jacob, learned he had been willed the farm, and because he disapproved utterly of 'exploiting animals' had refused to take over the running of the place. To solve this problem, or, in Dolly's opinion, to get out from under, Jack had divided the property into shares.

His mother had got one share, his brother Joe another, his grandfather Sam Pearson a third, his sister Peggy a fourth, and he himself had retained the last share. Grandad, not wishing the responsibility of the shareholder's role, had sold out to Henry Wilks, which was a lucky thing for Emmerdale because Henry had business acumen as well as funds in the bank.

Matt had inherited his share on the death of his first wife Peggy. He never really thought of himself as a shareholder. He had been a farm worker at Emmerdale when he and Peggy got married, he liked the job, he considered himself a farm worker still. When called upon to make decisions in committee for Emmerdale Farm Limited, he gave from his experience as a farm worker, shepherd, and cowman. The business side he left exclusively to Henry.

Only recently, at the urging of Dolly, had he begun to argue his own case. But so far it had been to improve the arrangements with which he did his job, not for himself but the animals. He had made a doughty stand for the sheep shelter and won, hands down, in face of Jack's intention to throw money away on one of his organic farming schemes. He would confront Jack on matters to do with the welfare of the animals – but not for himself.

'What did Ma say about it all?' Dolly asked.

'She were upset, you could see that. But she . . . well, she wants her grandson living at Emmerdale, love. Anything that will improve the chance of getting young Jackie here is what she supports. And of course you have to understand, Jack's her first-born.'

'Um,' said Dolly. Being herself pregnant, she must have

sympathy with any woman's affection for her child. All the same, she said to herself, I hope our son's not going to be as self-centred as Jack Sugden. Aloud she remarked, 'Annie doesn't go along with all Jack's daft ideas, even so.'

'But this isn't a daft idea, lass! It's a right grand idea! Trouble is, Jack spoke up first.' He sighed. 'You wanted us to announce the plan . . . I should have listened to you.'

'Oh, Matt!' She put her arms around him and gave him a fierce little hug. 'Now don't you go blaming yourself. How could anybody foresee Jack would come up with it? It's just bad luck he did. But . . . it's not bad luck that he got the better of the argument over it. I feel somebody ought to have spoke up for us. Didn't anyone say we ought to have the barn? Not even Henry? I'd have thought Henry'd be on our side – he's learned enough of Jack to know where Emmerdale's success depends.'

'It weren't a question of sides, love. It were a matter of being practical. When Jack and Pat are married, there'll be three more bodies to find beds for –'

'Nay, Pat'll go into Jack's room, surely. It's only the two kids they have to find beds for.' Despite herself, Dolly couldn't help a bit of a roguish smile at this.

Seeing her mood lightening, Matt went along with this aspect of the conversation. 'All right, the two kids. There just aren't the rooms available.'

'There'd be our room if we had the barn.'

'That's one room. But Jackie and Sandie can hardly share it, now can they?'

'So how about when I've got the baby? How will we manage that?'

'A baby don't need a room to itself –'

'Not at first. But the time'll come, won't it?'

'We'll have to start looking again, that's all.' He got up and offered her his hand to pull her up. 'Come on, let's go and get that drink. Cheer us up.'

She let herself be pulled up so that she was against his chest. She looked up into his face, gave a little smile, and he kissed her on the cheek. They began to move off towards the lane. 'Other farms provide cottages for their workers. Couldn't Emmerdale think along those lines?'

'I've always been part of the family at Emmerdale,

Dolly.'

'I know,' she sighed. 'That's part of t'trouble . . .'

'Nay, nay, lass. I'd not have it different. I like being part of the family.'

And so did she. Her relationship with Annie was close and almost daughterlike. Yet there were times when she longed to be on her own with Matt, to be able to loll in an armchair across the hearthrug from him, to cook the meals he liked best, to spend an evening with a dress pattern spread out all across the floor and not inconvenience anyone but herself . . .

At the Woolpack they encountered Joe. He arrived in the N.Y. Estates Land-Rover, saw them, and came to commiserate before going into the pub to get his drink. They were sitting at a trestle table in the open air, savouring the scent of the lilac blooming in Mrs Tyler's cottage garden a few doors down.

'I'm sorry the barn conversion didn't work out for you,' he said.

'Thanks, Joe.'

'I'd have liked to do summat to help the argument but Jack is marrying a family, not just a single woman. I suppose he's got to have somewhere to live.'

Dolly looked straight at him. 'How about taking them in at Demdyke?'

Demdyke was a little terraced cottage which Joe had bought about three years previously, when the need to get away from the cares of the job as farm manager at Emmerdale had seemed paramount. It hadn't been much of a place when he bought it and, bachelorlike, he'd done very little to it so it still wasn't much of a place. All the same, he lived there alone.

Matt had put a restraining hand on Dolly. 'Hey-up, lass,' he objected.

'But there's only Joe in it, and he just said he'd like to do summat.'

'And I would – but you'd hardly fit Jack and Pat and two teenagers in there. It's only two up and one down – it'd mean young Jackie kipping on the sofa in the living-room all the time and I can't see that being greeted with delight.'

Dolly looked as if she felt it might be greeted with some

24

enthusiasm by someone else – namely herself – if Joe would just offer it. But when she thought of it she saw it raised yet another problem: where would Joe live? He certainly wouldn't want to get a room at Home Farm, the headquarters of N.Y. Estates. It would mean living on top of his boss, Alan Turner, the general manager, a man of whom it could be said as Wordsworth had it, 'there were few to know and very few to love'. Turner was a first rate flannel-merchant – as friendly as a spaniel at first encounter, yet once you got to know him you realized he was devious and selfseeking.

Joe wouldn't want to live in the same house as Turner. Besides, most of the rooms at Home Farm were now in use for storage. Only the central wing of the house was liveable – and Alan Turner would probably not welcome a live-in assistant who could keep an eye on all his little ways.

The only other way Demdyke could become available was if Joe would go back to live at Emmerdale. But that was equally unwelcome as an idea to Joe. N.Y. Estates wouldn't take kindly to their farm manager living in the house of one of their chief critics and antagonists; the manager of Emmerdale. Besides, it would be asking for trouble for Joe to be living in the farmhouse with Jack a few yards away in the old barn. They'd be at each other's throats in no time.

No, it was no good having pipe dreams of that kind. She would have to resign herself to the fact that although there was accommodation, somehow none of it sorted itself out to be of any help to her and Matt.

She came back to earth to find that Joe and Matt were discussing how rooms might be swapped round at Emmerdale. 'Ma won't mind having Sandie share with her, I s'pose. It's the obvious thing. But what are they going to do wi' Jackie?'

'Goodness knows. And he's a difficult lad, you know, Matt. Ma doesn't want to believe it, but Jackie's no angel by a long chalk.'

'We're all going to have to be a bit angelic if we're not going to get on each other's nerves,' Dolly observed.

'You can say that again!' Joe sighed gustily. 'Listen, tell you what. I could ask Alan to let you have Tolly's farmhouse. How about that?'

'Joe! Would you?'

'Hang on, Dolly,' Matt said, quick to check unfounded hopes. 'Tolly's is N.Y. property. Why should they offer it to us when they could use it for their own workers?'

'Alan offered it to Pat and Jack.'

'He what?'

'Well . . . one of his generous moods . . . Pat being on our staff as a clerk in the office –'

'But she's only part-time, Joe,' Dolly put in, trying to grapple with it. Then, finding that very fact hopeful, she went on: 'Well, if he would offer it to Pat when she's only part-time, why shouldn't he offer it to us?'

'No reason, as far as I can see. Jack wouldn't take the house, because of course he didn't want to be beholden to N.Y. Estates.'

'Of course,' said Dolly with some sarcasm.

Joe was trying to work out the politics of Turner's offer of the house. He was pretty sure it had been done for exactly the reasons his brother suspected – to put Jack under an obligation so he wouldn't be any further trouble. The stated reason – that Pat had a right to be offered a house since she was an N.Y. employee – was really quite flimsy.

Predictably, Jack had said no. Turner had been quite miffed. 'I made the offer in good faith,' he mourned to Joe. 'I do wish your brother wouldn't be so suspicious all the time.'

As far as Joe could work it out, Turner might let Matt have the house for just the same reason – to put Emmerdale under an obligation. From Turner's point of view it ought to work just as well – better, perhaps. It would be less blatant than toadying to the farm manager of Emmerdale himself. Doing a good turn to one of his workers was somehow more generous and open-hearted. Yes, there was a good chance Alan would go for it.

He knew he had to choose his moment for suggesting the idea to Turner. At the moment there was a bit of a flap on at Home Farm. They were short of labour, so Turner was negotiating the loan of a man from HQ in Lincolnshire. Joe held his peace about the subject until everything settled down towards a peaceful ending to hay and silage making, explaining to Matt that it didn't do to rush into a thing like this at the wrong moment.

Life was hectic at Emmerdale too, for there were only ten days left before the wedding. Jack had put absolutely no thought into the ceremony itself beyond finding a minister in Hotten who was glad to give a blessing on the marriage – this to please Pat, for Jack was quite indifferent about religion in its formal sense. But he hadn't thought much about the temporary sleeping arrangements either. It apparently hadn't occurred to him that in his room, which Pat would have to share until the barn was ready for occupation, there was only a single bed.

Annie tried to talk to him about these matters. As usual he seemed to think life would arrange itself without effort if only they took things in their stride. He didn't want a reception, he hadn't thought about where Jackie would sleep, he didn't intend to invite anyone to the ceremony. His plan seemed to be to go to Hotten Registry, commandeer two passers-by for witnesses, go to the church for the blessing, and make off straight away for a long weekend as a honeymoon.

Well, Annie simply wasn't having that. She took matters in hand. A small reception was arranged at Emmerdale, Joe was invited to be best man, and due to tactful handling Grandad agreed to share his bedroom temporarily with his great-grandson Jackie. Annie turned out a tiny boxroom for Sandie – a mere cubbyhole, really, which she was half ashamed to offer the girl.

Sandie, for her part, was delighted by it. It was better than sharing a bedroom with Mum at the caravan, tiny as it was. It had a narrow window high up in the wall which let in enough daylight for her to do her homework by. Her shy delight when she settled in was charming to see. Annie felt a surge of warmth for the child. She'd had a difficult life so far. Perhaps here at Emmerdale everything would blossom for her.

Jackie was a different matter. He wasn't ill-mannered to the Emmerdale family, he was simply cool. If he had been asked in the confessional to explain his feelings towards them, he'd have said he admired and respected Annie, liked Matt, thought Dolly was a bit of all right, and could perhaps get fond of Great-Grandad. But as for his father – his real father, as people phrased it, though to Jackie it still seemed unreal – the boy was fixed in unremitting dislike. He scarcely exchanged a word with him, and when he did it was usually rebellious.

The wedding took place in a glow of optimism and good wishes. Off went Pat and Jack to their secret destination for three days' honeymoon. Those remaining behind settled back to take up their daily lives again.

Joe was introduced to Teddy Hooson, who'd been sent from Spalding to drive the tractor for hay-making. 'Hooson?' he repeated as they nodded a greeting at each other. 'You'll be Harry Hooson's son, then? Bye, you've changed since last I saw you!'

Teddy grinned and flexed his shoulders. 'Good living and regular hours,' he remarked. He was a well-set-up young man who looked a bit older than his eighteen years. 'They said in Spalding you were a bit pushed over the hay harvest?'

'Aye, we've had all kinds o' trouble – machine breakdowns, shortage of labour . . .'

'Want me to start right in now?'

Joe was surprised at the offer. It was almost nine o'clock at night and though the light was still good and the weather dry, volunteering to get up on the driving cab the minute he got in from Spalding showed an unexpected keenness. Then it occurred to him that of course it would mean overtime pay. He shook his head. 'Nay, the other men will be knocking off in half an hour. N.Y.'s policy is not to overdo the long hours – wives don't like it too well, sitha. And by the time I'd shown you your machine and you'd got up on the field, it'd be getting dim light. But you could plunge straight in tomorrow, eh?'

'You're the boss,' agreed Hooson, pleased at the thought of Sunday double-time.

Joe felt he ought to do a little to make the lad feel welcome. 'Come on down to the Woolpack and I'll buy you a welcome drink,' he suggested. 'It's a long time since you've been there, quite like a homecoming!'

Henry Wilks only just recognized Hooson. He could tell it was someone he'd formerly seen about the village but couldn't get the name. 'Teddy Hooson,' Joe introduced. 'Pull us a half each, Henry. He's our replacement tractor driver.'

'Tractor driving, is it? My, my, you've done well, lad.'

'That's why I left Beckindale,' Hooson explained. 'Learn tractor driving and better meself.' He glanced about with tolerant amusement. 'This place ain't changed much.'

'And why should it?' Amos Brearly enquired, coming to the bar from the back room. 'When you've got the best, you stick to it.'

'Couldn't have phrased it better myself,' said Henry.

Amos was eyeing the newcomer. 'You're Teddy Hooson, aren't you?' he asked threateningly.

'That's right sir, guilty as charged, and I'm having a half-pint of your best bitter.'

'Oh are you! Well, first tell me –'

'How old are you now then?' said Teddy, and in chorus with him came another young voice, that of Jackie Merrick.

Everyone laughed – except Amos, who glared at them all. 'Very funny. Now answer the question.'

'Heck, Amos, he must be coming on nineteen!' said Joe.

'You may know that. I don't, and I've my licence to think on.'

'I was eighteen last October the eighteenth – satisfied?'

'You can serve him, Mr Wilks,' Amos said in a tone of generosity, and moved off to clear dirty glasses.

'Always the same,' Jackie declared. 'The day Amos lets you have a drink without a hassle, that's the day you're entitled to vote!'

Joe performed introductions then left the two youngsters to get to know each other. It seemed to him they'd have more in common than he and Teddy. To tell the truth, he didn't altogether take to Teddy. Some instinct made him regard the lad with less than enthusiasm.

All the same, he proved a competent worker, good with machinery. The hay-making was soon almost completed but

Alan Turner having asked to keep Teddy for a couple of weeks, he put the lad on potato-spraying. 'You know how to handle a sprayer?' Joe asked him.

'Oh aye. Nowt to it.'

'And how to use a chart for the application rate?'

'I've done all that at Spalding,' Teddy said with a tinge of impatience.

'Good for you,' said Turner, who was taking part in this mini-conference about how best to use Teddy. Turner was pleased with his acquisition. He'd had to argue strongly to get him, and it was good to have a young, proficient craftsman on their strength. 'It means you can make your own hours as long as you get the job done, Hooson. Right?'

'Right. What tractor shall I take?'

'You can't start right away, I'm afraid,' Joe put in. 'The di-methoate hasn't arrived.'

Turner looked annoyed, his florid face creasing in resentment. 'You said it was due the day before yesterday!' he accused.

'So it was. But it's not here.'

'Have you been on to them?'

'There's a strike,' Joe said flatly.

'Dear God!' It was clear Turner was inclined to blame the strike on Joe. He turned to Teddy. 'Get off and help pick up the bales we're going to stack. You might as well do something now you're free.'

'What field?' Teddy asked.

'I'll take you up.' But Joe was stopped as he moved towards the Land-Rover.

'Just a minute, Joe.' Turner jerked his head at Teddy. 'Go and wait by the Land-Rover. I want a word with Joe.' He waited until Teddy had walked a few paces away before he went on. 'When did you know about this strike, Joe?'

'Yesterday.'

'Why didn't you let me know? I had to practically go on my knees to borrow that lad and now we don't need him.'

'We'll need him as soon as t' strike finishes.'

'And when's that likely to be, for God's sake? It could be weeks.'

Joe was a little indignant. Turner was always putting him somehow in the wrong. 'All the more reason to have him handy,' he said. 'The longer the strike goes on, the quicker we'll need him on the spraying when it's over. There's only a couple of weeks in which it's any use spraying potatoes – '

'I do know that, thanks, Joe,' Turner said in a cool tone. 'But if I had known the di-methoate was going to be delayed, I could have scheduled the work differently.'

'Listen, what do you want from me?' Joe broke in in exasperation. 'I didn't know there was going to be a strike any more than you did. If you think it's a waste having Teddy hanging about, then send him back to Spalding.'

'But then if the strike's over quickly I'll have to go begging for him again.'

'Well, so what? If they want the farms run properly it's up to them to supply the labour. They can't expect us to work miracles, especially when outside circumstances affect us suddenly.'

As always when he got opposition, Turner began back-pedalling hastily. 'All right, Joe, no need to get het up. I'm only thinking of our image with the big brass. Don't want to put up a black. I wasn't blaming you.'

'It sounded like it to me!'

'Then I apologize. But let's be practical. Can we find an alternative supply of di-methoate?'

'I'm trying. But the strike's at the rail depot and there seems no way of getting round it.'

'Somebody must have stocks, surely?'

Joe said, enjoying the remark, 'You fixed it with Abbots instead of Millers because the bulk buying discount was better. I think Millers have stocks, though.'

Immediately Turner began his tactical withdrawal. 'Well, it's not desperate, just awkward . . . You get off and I'll see if I can do anything on the old boy network.'

'I wish you luck. I tried Millers – they said regular customers had first claim.'

'Oh, there's ways and means,' Turner said, building up his own confidence. 'I'll see you later if there's nothing else to arrange.'

'There is one thing,' said Joe, feeling that here was a moment when he had the advantage over the wily estate manager.

'Yes? If it's your salary review, that's not until –'

'Nay, it's nowt like that. You remember that place you were offering to Pat Merrick and our Jack?'

'Tolly Farmhouse. Yes, what about it? Don't tell me they want it after all?' Joe could see Turner's little wheels whizzing round as he calculated how much good this might do him at HQ.

'No, they're fixed up otherwise. But are you going to let Tolly's or what?'

'That depends.'

'On what?'

'On why you're asking.'

'Well . . .' Joe took a deep breath and plunged in. He wasn't exactly keen on what he was about to do. It was going to put him under a personal obligation to Turner if Turner agreed to help Matt Skilbeck. And one of the last things Joe wanted was to have to be grateful to Alan Turner. All the same, he'd promised Dolly and Matt. 'You know Matt Skilbeck up at Emmerdale?'

'Of course I do! Wins awards at the shows for his sheep. I hear nothing but good of him. And married to that nice girl . . . what's her name again?'

'Dolly.'

'She's got a lot of charm. A nice couple.' This fulsome praise was due to the fact that Turner quite admired Dolly, and if the truth were told thought she was wasted on slow, unadventurous Matt Skilbeck.

'They're looking for somewhere to live, have been for quite a while. Dolly's expecting, and they'd like a place of their own –'

'That's only reasonable.'

'I wondered if you'd let them have Tolly's?'

'Ah,' said Turner. A pause ensued.

'Well?' Joe prompted.

'I can't give an answer off the cuff like this, Joe.'

'Why not?'

'Well, it depends on what plans, if any, Headquarters have for the place.'

Joe was vexed. 'If you were going to let Pat and Jack have it, you must have understood they didn't have any plans for it.'

'That's a little different. Pat works here. HQ would agree there's no argument about allowing one of our own employees to have the lease of one of our properties. But I don't know how they'd react to seeing it taken by a complete outsider.'

Joe hesitated. Was it better to let well alone, or to push a little? He decided on a little flannelling on his own initiative. 'They're hard pushed, you see, at Emmerdale. Need more space . . .'

'Of course. And with a new baby coming . . .' Turner thought for a moment then looked sympathetic. 'Leave it with me, Joe,' he murmured. 'I'll see what I can do.'

'Thanks,' said Joe. 'They'll be grateful.' He was pleased. He'd learned that it paid to think twice when you were discussing anything with Turner, and on this occasion it seemed to have worked. He'd yet to learn that it paid to think three times.

Teddy Hooson, having been taken up to look at the field where he'd be picking up hay bales, went back to Home Farm to hitch the loader to the tractor. Jackie Merrick came to take a look. 'Like that kind of thing, do you?' he enquired. 'Working with machines?'

'The coming thing, they are,' Teddy said over his shoulder as he finished completing the hitch. 'More future in it than in looking after pheasant chicks.'

'Dunno so much. If they go on automating farms like they do, they'll soon have an army of robots – not folk at all. Won't even need clever dicks like you driving 'em.'

'Ha.' Teddy straightened, rubbed his chin. 'Not far off dinnertime, eh? Hardly worth going up to start on the field just to knock off for me dinner. You going to the pub?'

Jackie shook his head. 'Promised Sandie I'd meet her at the caravan, sort out what we're going to take to Emmerdale permanent and what we're going to junk.'

'Sandie? That's your sister, right? What's she like?'

Jackie shrugged. 'She's all right. Come and meet her, if you like.'

Since Mr Turner had told him to work the tractor to his own schedule, Teddy decided that he had plenty of time to go to the caravan and meet Jackie Merrick's sister, go on afterwards to the Woolpack for a pint and a pie, and still be well within his lunchtime allowance. He set off at Jackie's side, dwarfed a little by the lankiness of the other boy but, in his opinion, considerably more worth looking at because of his new T-shirt and tight jeans and his well-cut hair. Jackie was rather impressed by Teddy. He earned good money at his trade. And it was clear he knew how to spend it.

At the caravan they found Sandie rooting around in a cardboard carton full of books. 'This is Teddy Hooson,' Jackie said. He didn't bother to introduce Sandie since it was clear who she was. Sandie nodded abstractedly at Teddy, her attention on her books.

'Have you thrown anything out since we left?' she accused Jackie.

'Nay, why should I? Haven't had time to get near the place.'

'Somebody's taken my algebra book.'

'Now that was probably the Pink Panther,' Teddy suggested. 'Just the kind of thing he'd go after, an algebra book.'

'The Pink Panther wasn't a man, it was a diamond,' Sandie said, pausing in her search to look at Teddy more keenly.

'Oh, was it? I forget. Saw the film, did you?'

'Yes. Really funny.'

'Like the flicks, do you?'

She shrugged. 'I generally have homework.'

'Homework?'

'Oh, she's a big brain,' Jackie said, in a mixture of pride and contempt. 'Doing A levels and all that.'

'Fancy that. Need any help with it?' said Teddy, grinning.

'Think you know any algebra?'

'Sure thing. Top of the class, I was. Twice y equals x – never got it wrong. Two x Teddy, they used to call me. Two exes for excellence.'

Sandie laughed. 'If you can do algebra as well as you blow your own trumpet, you should be a whizz.' She turned to her brother. 'Come on, Jackie, let's get this done. I'm on a free period at the moment but I've got to be back for science practical at two-thirty.'

Despite himself, Teddy was impressed. He didn't usually like clever girls, who tended to be snooty and difficult to impress. But Sandie's little dark face, her slight figure, her soft light voice and quick wits, were a combination he found very pleasing. Besides, a quick run-down of the talent in Beckindale during a long and boring Sunday evening had already convinced him she was the best available source of amusement.

'Can I do anything?' he enquired, elbowing his way into the caravan.

'Nay, we've just got to look through a few things.'

'You could make us all a cup of coffee,' Sandie suggested. 'This is my lunch hour really.'

Jackie was somehow a little annoyed at this quick offer of hospitality to Teddy, but had some concern for his sister. 'You had owt to eat?'

'I've got a sandwich here – Mrs Sugden made it for me this morning.' She took it out of her shoulder bag, unwrapped it, showing it to be two rounds of home-made bread with a handsome filling of ham.

'Bye!' Teddy said. 'Catering's good at your establishment.'

'Want a bit?'

'Nay, Sandie, Teddy's going to have a pie at the Woolpack,' Jackie said. He looked pointedly at Teddy. 'Won't you be a bit late back at work if you hang around here drinking coffee and then get your food at the Woolpack?'

'He could have some of my –'

'Mrs Sugden made that for *you*,' Jackie said with considerable firmness. 'Now come on, Teddy, Joe'll be looking for you.'

'Oh, a bit of a tartar, is he, Joe Sugden?'

'He's all right,' Jackie said with a shrug. 'But you've only been at N.Y. five minutes. You don't want to blot your copybook, do you?'

'Heaven forbid,' Teddy said in a tone that implied he didn't care in the least. 'Okay then, see you in the Woolpack when you've finished here?'

'Happen,' said Jackie.

Teddy leapt out of the van and down the steps to the

35

ground with a little display like a circus acrobat. 'Ally-oop,' he said cheerfully. 'See you around, Sandie.'

When he had gone Sandie looked at her brother. 'You didn't need to chase him off like that!'

'Never mind him. What about this book of yours?' In the search for it, Teddy Hooson was momentarily forgotten.

At that moment Alan Turner had at last got through to Headquarters in Spalding. There had been a busy signal for over half an hour. Now a brisk secretarial voice said, 'You're through to Mr Norris,' and Norris said in his usual indifferent tone: 'Yes?'

It was one of the chief aims of Turner's life to impress Cyril Norris.

'Ah, glad to get you at last,' he began. 'Listen, Norris, am I right in thinking I'm one under strength on the labour front here at Beckindale?'

'If it's about Hooson, I agreed you could –'

'No, no, he's all right. I've not been able to use him on spraying today as I intended because of some problem over di-methoate.'

'Really, Turner, you're expected to sort out things like that for yourself!'

'That's not why I'm ringing,' Turner replied. 'It's about our staffing problems. We'll be losing Jesse Gillan in the autumn when he retires. Well, I think I've found just the man we need to replace him.'

'A shepherd? There are plenty of those about.'

'Not winners at county shows.'

'Oh?' There came a faint difference in Norris's voice. 'You've got a show winner?'

'Not exactly got him.' Turner decided to do himself a bit of good. 'It will need some tact and diplomacy to get him on our strength –'

'Tact and diplomacy? Offer him a good wage!'

'That wouldn't do it in this case, Norris. No, it will be a case of softly-softly here, but I think I can do it.'

'Bully for you if you do,' Norris said with just the slightest evidence of enthusiasm. 'Always good to have another feather in your cap, eh?'

'That's what I thought.'

36

Turner rang off feeling understandably pleased with himself. Actually got that stick Norris to sound interested! Now all he had to do was catch his hare – and he knew just how to do that.

Chapter Three

Jack Sugden and his wife arrived home from their honeymoon about mid-morning of the next day, Tuesday. Although everyone tried to be welcoming, it was still rather a restrained homecoming. No question of carrying the bride over the threshold, for instance. Annie was preparing mid-morning coffee, Matt was just indoors for a break from a session of hay-stacking, and Grandad was washing his hands at the sink after a hard hour's gardening.

'Welcome, love,' Annie said, giving Pat a kiss on the cheek. 'You're just right for coffee.'

'Been getting on all right without me?' Jack asked cheerily.

'Biscuit or cake with your coffee?' Dolly enquired.

Pat looked at her with something like timidity. She knew how she herself would feel towards a woman who had stepped in and commandeered the home she'd been picturing. 'Whichever's easiest . . .'

'Nay, be a devil and have cake,' Dolly said, relenting. After all, it wasn't really Pat's fault.

'After we've had it we'll go out and take a walk around, just to see how everything's looking,' Jack suggested. 'Then I'll get down to it. Get an hour in afore dinnertime.'

He and Pat set out arm in arm through the gate in the back wall of the farm's outer yard, still a little strange in their new relationship. Pat's son, Jackie, was just emerging from a copse on the edge of N.Y.'s land as they breasted the rise bordering Emmerdale. Jackie put a hand on Teddy Hooson's arm and drew him back into the shelter of the hazel bushes.

'Hey-up, what's wrong?' Teddy objected.

'I don't want 'em to see me.'

'What for? We've only been looking at the traps, not

37

poaching!'

'I don't want to meet him when he's with me Mum.'

Teddy peered out between the bushes. 'It's Jack Sugden, isn't it?'

'Oh, you know him, do you?'

''Course I know him. Quite famous, he is.'

Jackie grunted. After a moment he stepped out of cover. 'It's all right, they've gone.'

Teddy followed, frowning. 'What does your Dad say to all that?'

'Me Dad?'

'Well, that Jack Sugden was arm in arm wi' her. Doesn't your Dad think it's a bit off?'

Jackie realized the other lad had spoken in complete innocence. The rising anger within him was curbed. 'Me Mum and Jack Sugden have just got wed,' he said. 'Didn't you hear in the village?'

'Oh . . . aye . . .' remembered Teddy. 'Didn't pay attention. Your Ma a widow, then?'

'Divorced.'

Although Teddy Hooson liked to think he was thoroughly sophisticated, he was still enough of a Beckindaler to find that faintly shocking. 'Never!' he muttered.

'Oh, it's been quite a poppyshow,' Jackie told him. His tone was hard and careless. 'You'd hear about it soon enough any road so I may as well tell you. My Ma got a divorce and just got married to Jack Sugden. And as anybody'll tell you if you give 'em half a chance, Jack Sugden's my real Dad – so now you know.'

'Your *real* Dad?' Teddy was genuinely staggered.

Jackie shrugged.

'And he just married her? Left it a bit late, didn't he?'

'He did,' Jackie said, 'and I hate his guts for it. And now shut up about it.'

Teddy had enough sense to take that advice. In any case it was time he got back to the tractor, which was at the last stages of hauling hay bales to the dutch barn. But later he took the trouble to be at the end of the lane leading to Emmerdale, just as Sandie was coming home from school.

'What are you doing here?' she greeted him, although

38

she knew.

'Waiting for you.'

'What for?'

'To see if you fancied coming out tonight.'

She considered. 'Where?'

'Where you like,' he said in a grand tone. 'Movie in Hotten? Or I hear there's a disco in the village tonight. Or we could just go for a walk. I don't mind.'

'Dunno. I've got homework to do.'

That was what he had expected her to say. 'Well, it's not going to take you all night, is it? Get it done quick, say by seven, eh?' He tapped his wrist watch. 'I'll call for you then. Okay?'

Although she was tempted, Sandie couldn't give in as quickly as that. 'There's no buses to Hotten after seven,' she told him. 'I expect you've forgotten, after being away.'

Teddy knew he was about to play his master card. 'I've got a car.'

It was all Sandie could do to hide the respect this information elicited. A car! One or two of the senior boys at school had a car, but so far none of them had shown any interest in her. To have a boyfriend with a car was considered the height of sophistication. What a triumph to be able to report it tomorrow to her classmates: 'Teddy drove me into Hotten last night in his car, so we could take in a movie . . .'

'Some old banger, is it?' she enquired with a lot of coolness.

'Lovely job. Wait till you see it.'

'Why didn't you bring it here to show me?'

''Cos I'm working.' He jerked a thumb towards the fields over his shoulder. 'My tractor's waiting over the back. Is it a date?'

Sandie considered honour had been satisfied and she could now agree. 'All right,' she said, 'if Mum'll let me.'

'Mum!' cried Teddy. 'How old are you, for heaven's sake?'

'Sixteen.'

'You're your own boss, then,' he told her. 'See you at seven.'

'But listen, Teddy –'

He didn't want to hear any ifs or buts. 'Can't wait,' he exclaimed, hastening away. 'I'm supposed to be working.'

Sandie looked after him with appreciation. He was a lively one. Not like most of the boys in Beckindale. He knew what he wanted, intended to get it. He'd moved away to Spalding to train with N.Y. Estates – that showed a lot of initiative. Yes, he was interesting, was Teddy Hooson.

She settled down as soon as she got indoors to do her homework. Tea wasn't until five-thirty, which gave her half an hour, and then after tea there would be about an hour – well, no, because she'd have to wash and do her hair and change . . .

All went well until she reached the point where she was in her second-best blouse and jeans, with her hair tied back in a black ribbon leaving little wisps at her cheeks. Her mother looked in surprise as she hovered about the door of the farmhouse.

'What are you all dressed up for?' she enquired. Now that Sandie had that little room of her own, it was possible for the girl to get ready to go out without its being noticed.

'Got a date.'

'Oh? With Andy?'

'No.'

'Well, who?' Pat asked, a little exasperated.

Sandie remembered Teddy's surprise when she had wondered if her Mum would let her go out. She bridled a little. 'His name's Teddy Hooson and he's a tractor driver at N.Y. If you want to know all about him, ask Jackie – it was him introduced me to him.'

'Well, *I've* not been introduced to him! Jackie!'

Jackie came to join them. By this time Sandie, in her anxiety to ensure she really would get out for the evening, had stepped out into the yard. Jackie came out. 'What's up?' he asked.

'Do you know this feller Harry Hooson?'

'Teddy Hooson,' he corrected. 'Aye, what about it?'

'Sandie says she's got a date with him.'

Jackie smothered a grin. Fast worker, Teddy. He waited for what was to follow.

'I mean, I've never even met the boy! What's he like?' his mother demanded.

40

'Seems all right to me. Got a good job, any road.'

'And that's something nowadays,' Sandie put in eagerly, knowing that her mother was always worried about finance and security.

'You're only sixteen, Sandie. Whether the boy has a safe job or not is hardly the point! What I want to know is, is he a nice lad? I mean, how long have you known him?'

'Oh, *Mum!*' It was the age-old cry of the daughter confronting a fussy old mother. 'What's that got to do with it? He's living here in Beckindale, he's working for N.Y. Jackie likes him. Do I have to meet him at church before I can make a date wi' him?'

Sandie had set off down the lane. Pat was just beginning: 'That's all very well . . .' when there was the roar of a car-engine at lane-end and an ancient open-topped car, painted in garish colours, jerked to a stop.

'Teddy!' cried Sandie in delight.

Pat was staring in amazement at the car, which looked more like something from a kid's space comic than a means of transport on British roads. Sandie ran to its side. Teddy opened the offside door for her.

'Hop in,' he said.

'Sandie!' cried Pat.

'It's all right, I'll look after her.'

'Is that your car?' Pat asked, hurrying towards him.

'Yeh, beauty, isn't she? Can't stop, film starts at half-past. By-ee.' He was gone in a grating of gears and a cloud of exhaust.

Pat rounded on Jackie. 'You introduced her to him, did you? You want your head examining!'

'Oh, come on, Ma! Just because he's painted up his car a bit fancy –'

'He wouldn't even wait to listen to what I wanted to say.'

'You wanted to tell him to get her back by ten o'clock, right?'

'Well . . .'

'Ma, the film doesn't finish till ten-thirty. 'Course he didn't want to hear you say she'd got to have an early night. Come on, he's only taking her to Hotten for a flick.' He hung a careless arm around her shoulders in comfort. 'You never mind when she goes out on her own with Andy

41

Longthorn.'

'But I know Andy Longthorn . . .'

'Well, you'll soon know Teddy. 'S not as if he's going to disappear from the village tomorrow. He's based at Home Farm – you can chat to him any time you like.'

'Yes . . . you're right . . . I'm being silly.'

Sandie, flying along the road to Hotten in Teddy's chariot of fire, was in a state of delight. If she remembered that her mother had not been very pleased at the manner of her departure, she banished it from her mind. Teddy drove into the cinema car park, escorted her into the foyer, bought two tickets, invited her to choose sweets from the kiosk, and generally set out to look like a big spender. He knew how to impress the chicks.

The film was rotten. Teddy felt it as a personal affront. He kept hoping it would improve but after an hour he was fed up with Roman generals posturing and Saxon maidens being led around in chains. 'Let's split,' he whispered in Sandie's ear. 'This is about as interesting as cold fish and chips.'

'Where'll we go?' she whispered back.

He knew better than to suggest a session in the car in the car park. She'd only just let him put his arm round her shoulders in the cinema. 'What about that disco in Beckindale?'

'I don't mind.'

Jackie was surprised to see them when they walked into the church hall. 'Hullo, what happened to the film?'

'Died in a chariot race,' Teddy said. 'Thought there might be more action here.'

The music on the turntable was reggae. He and Sandie began to move to the heavy rhythm. 'Owt to drink here?' he asked over his shoulder to a neighbouring dancer.

'Lemonade, coke . . .'

'Oh, great,' groaned Teddy who, since he was first allowed to order bitter in a pub, had never drunk anything less strong.

His thirst wouldn't be satisfied with lemonade. Besides, you didn't get anywhere with a bird by feeding her lemonade. 'How about a quick one before the Woolpack shuts?'

'I can't go to the pub,' Sandie reminded him. 'I'm under age.'

'No problem. We'll go down the Woolpack in the car, I park it up the back and go get us drinks to have in the car, nice and cosy.'

Sandie hesitated. She didn't want to appear naive by saying it sounded the kind of thing Mum would disapprove of.

'They'll be turning us out of here soon anyway,' Teddy urged. 'Finishes at half-ten, doesn't it?'

While she was still trying to make up her mind to say yes or no, he led her out. As they reached the door the vicar said gently, 'Goodnight, Sandie. Hope you enjoyed it.'

'Great,' Teddy replied in his slickest tones, 'get it like this in church and you'll have me there praying.'

Sandie saw the hurt flash into Hinton's eyes but before she could apologize Teddy had drawn her through the doorway and out to his car.

'You shouldn't have said that to him,' she rebuked as she got in. 'He's nice, Mr Hinton.'

'Oh, then I'll apologize next time I see him. My experience is, most clergymen are dead from the neck up.'

'Mr Hinton's not like that.'

'Well, good for him.' In no time at all they were at the pub. Teddy went briskly in, bought a can of lager for himself and a shandy for the girl.

Sandy had been expecting Seven-up or Schweppes. 'There's alcohol in this, isn't there?' she said doubtfully.

'Ooh, yes, enough to cover a halfpence piece, I shouldn't wonder. Come on, drink up.'

Sandie tasted it. It seemed to be mostly lime cordial. She couldn't exactly say she liked it, but it wasn't bad. Seeing Teddy eyeing her with amusement, she took several big swallows.

'That's the girl,' he encouraged. 'It's an acquired taste. Like, when you're a kid, you like sweet things – strawberry jam and honey. But as you get older you cultivate a taste for interesting things like bitter marmalade.'

'Or caviar,' supplied Sandie. '"Caviar to the general" – that's in Shakespeare.'

43

'You can be sure generals get all the good things,' Teddy agreed.

'No, no, it means –'

'What I always say,' he went on, putting an arm over her shoulder, 'is that a little of what you fancy does you good. Like a bit of cosiness on a cool night like this.' He tried to edge closer.

'I think you'd better drive me home,' Sandie said, resisting.

He shook his head. 'Have to drink up first. Otherwise it's a waste of money, isn't it?'

She gave a little shrug and tipped the can up at her lips again. Truth to tell, its contents did seem more agreeable, and moreover a slight haziness was coming over her that was not unpleasant.

'There's no hurry, is there?' Teddy went on. 'The night's young, and so are we, eh?' He'd heard that in a song on one of his Ma's old forty-fives. He'd found it a useful line on more than one occasion.

'But as a matter o' fact . . .' Sandie said, finding to her surprise that her tongue didn't quite seem to respond as it should, 'I'm younger than you, and my Mum . . .'

'She was young once too, you know,' he assured her. He turned her face towards him, took the can from her and placed it on the floor. He was just about to kiss her when headlights flashed at the bend of the road and a Land-Rover came round.

They started in guilty surprise and sat apart from each other. The Land-Rover, which had been going slowly because of the bend, came to a halt.

Jack Sugden, the driver, had seen the two quite clearly in his headlights. Frowning, he got out and walked to the side of the gaudy little car.

'What's this, Sandie?' he asked with some sternness.

He knew nothing about her date. He had gone out immediately after tea to consult a farmer the far side of Hotten about the making of organic compost in large enough quantities for agricultural use. One thing had led to another and instead of getting away within an hour, Jack had stayed to chat until well gone nine.

Teddy stared at him in resentment. 'What's it got to do

with you?' he said.

Jack ignored him. 'I think you should be home by now, Sandie, shouldn't you?'

'What you think is nothing to do with her,' Teddy cried, furious at being disregarded.

'I'll take you home now if you like?' said Jack to the girl.

'She's got transport,' Teddy said, starting his engine.

'Now just a minute!' At last Jack had to turn his attention to the boy. 'Her mother will be worried –'

'Oh aye?' sneered Teddy. 'From what I hear, you caused her Mum a bit of worry yourself!' Next moment he was gone.

Jack stood staring after the tail lights. Who on earth was that awful boy? And what on earth was Sandie doing out with him – and well after the time she knew her mother would want her indoors?

In the Woolpack, the sound of the car's exhaust-roar reached those sitting near the open windows. 'That sounds like a lawnmower cutting steel grass,' Matt said to Dolly.

She smiled. She knew he was trying to lighten the atmosphere.

Today had not been a good day for Dolly. Before Jack and Pat arrived home, she and Annie had had a long talk, which had started with the anxieties about the sleeping arrangements.

Needing to voice her despondency, Dolly had said: 'All this would be easier if me and Matt weren't here in the way, wouldn't it?'

Annie, setting extra towels ready to take upstairs, looked over her shoulder at her. There was a crease between her brows. 'Don't say that, lass,' she begged. 'It makes me feel that happen I've given you some reason to think you're not wanted.'

Dolly was quite calm. 'Nay, I didn't mean it that way, Ma. I was just facing facts. You want your daughter-in-law and her family here. I can understand that, it's perfectly natural.' She sighed. 'But you can't help seeing . . . I mean, everybody else here is family, is related –'

'That's not important –'

'It is, Annie. You don't see it because you're not in my

45

place. But it's how I feel. So when we began to realize what a crush there was going to be, me and Matt got the idea for the barn. That turned out to be a wash-out and it's made me see . . .' She paused. 'I really think it's time we left, Ma.'

She knew she had hurt Annie, but she didn't regret getting it out in the open. It was all very well for everyone to be making preparations to welcome Pat and Jack home, and finding room for Pat's two children, but she and Matt were on the outside looking in, to some extent. She'd had this feeling once before at a party, when her escort's car had broken down and they couldn't leave although their hosts were dying to get to bed. She had a sensation of having outstayed their welcome.

No matter how much Annie might argue against it, it was so. And when the newlyweds turned up and began talking blithely about their plans for the barn, she felt it all the more keenly.

Annie knew the atmosphere was a little strained. But more than that, she was distressed about the idea that Matt might want to leave. When he came in about mid-afternoon to telephone about the non-delivery of di-methoate to Emmerdale, she took the chance to speak to him.

There was no one else about. Dolly had gone to the village shop, Grandad was out in his workshop, Jack was on the far side of the twenty acre making up his mind whether to plough straight away or let the land breathe after the hay harvest, while Pat was over at the caravan clearing up.

'Matt . . .'

'Aye?' Matt said, replacing the telephone.

'Dolly told me you're going to look for somewhere else to live.'

He gave a slight frown. 'Well, we've done that afore.'

'Yes, but . . . We know there's nothing hard by. You'd go looking outside Beckindale?'

'Might have to.'

'Because of the barn?'

He shook his fair head. 'Not just that. Wi' the baby coming, it's best we have a place of our own. That's why we thought of the barn, of course. It sort of . . .' He hesitated. He couldn't bring himself to say that it had stuck in Dolly's throat, the ease with which it had been taken from them. 'What I mean is – we were thinking about the barn so we'd been serious about a place of our own before Jack got it.'

The simplicity of the statement robbed it of reproach. 'Jack got it' . . . there was the nub of the situation. Annie felt a twinge of conscience. They had been over-eager to reach a decision on that. It always seemed to be the way where Jack was concerned. Everything had to be decided in five minutes, and generally to his liking. She had gone along with it – she didn't excuse herself. And, when you came to think of it, what else could they have done? It was a way of fitting the Merrick family into Emmerdale.

But the thought of Matt and Dolly moving away was still hurtful.

'I'd best get on,' Matt said, seeing the distress in her eyes. He didn't want to stop and chew over the arguments – that got you nowhere. He'd come to believe that Dolly was right; it was time to have his own household.

That evening he'd found the atmosphere in the farm kitchen uncongenial. Jack had gone out on some harebrained visit to learn how to make compost for farming. Young Jackie had mooned about until it was time for the disco to start. Sandie was off somewhere with some young fellow and Pat was worried about it, continually getting up and going to the door, and looking up each time a car passed lane-end. Annie was finishing a sweater for Jackie. Grandad was reading the paper and complaining about the state of the world.

About nine o'clock he suggested to Dolly they should go out for some air and a nightcap in the Woolpack. She didn't really want a drink but she too was fed up with the crowded farm kitchen.

'Just let me get my cardy, love, it's turning cool.' Walking to the inn, he'd remarked that Annie was perturbed over what she'd been told that morning.

'She had to know some time, love.'

He nodded, hair glinting in the light of the half moon. 'Aye, aye . . . I realize that . . . I don't like the thought of hurting her feelings, though. And it *will* hurt her when we go. Well, I could see it had hurt her, just to hear of it.'

Dolly stopped and half-turned to him. 'I've got feelings too!' she exclaimed, emotion underlying the words.

'I know that, love. I don't mind you having told her, really, but you know how it is . . . Just the thought . . .'

'I don't want to hurt Annie either. But I think,' said Dolly in a quiet tone, 'she might have been a bit more on our side over the barn.'

'I think she –'

'She at least ought not to have let Jack get it so easy.'

'But Jack *is* the eldest son –'

'She's always saying you're one of the family. That was her chance to prove it, Matt.'

'You've got to realize she's always sort of got this fear that Jack'll just pack up and go. He's done it more'n once before.'

Dolly might have said she thought it might be no bad thing for Emmerdale if Jack did up-sticks again. But she knew that wouldn't do. Matt's loyalty wouldn't let him agree with her.

Jack was a factor in Dolly's life that caused her a lot of trouble. While she sympathized with his need to sort out his relationship, first with Pat and then, after the marriage, with his natural son Jackie, she found herself growing more and more aware of his faults. Why did he always have to consider himself and his conscience so much more important than anything else? Playing about with their livelihood because he disapproved of exploiting the land . . . As if Matt would ever 'exploit' anything! If Jack would only guide his conduct by Matt, he'd be a happier man.

The outing to the Woolpack wasn't a success. Neither of them cheered up very much. With the baby coming, they should have been full of hope as they looked forward, yet they were somehow heavy-hearted. When they got home, there would be the kitchen with everyone getting ready for bed, or perhaps still worrying about Sandie. And in the morning the same muddle and confusion over breakfast and getting first Jackie off to work and then Sandie off to school. And always Jack suggesting ideas to Pat about the conversion of the barn, oblivious of the fact that his every word hurt them.

*

Next morning in the milking parlour Jack and Matt were busy with their work and their own thoughts. But as they were clearing up about seven o'clock, Jack began asking what Matt knew of Teddy Hooson.

'N.Y. took on a few lads when they bought Verney's land. Teddy was one of 'em,' Matt recalled. 'I think he showed he had a bit of ambition so they sent him to Spalding to learn about tractors.'

'So he belongs at Spalding?'

'As far as I know. Jackie's a pal of his, I think – why don't you ask the lad?'

Jack said nothing. Matt regretted the suggestion. Jack couldn't ask young Jackie anything without getting a pert reply. 'Why're you interested in him anyway?'

'I came on him and young Sandie canoodling in a car last night. I told her to come home.'

'Canoodling?' Matt echoed with a little burst of laughter.

'It's nowt to laugh at, Matt. Sandie's only sixteen.'

'That's grown-up, these days. What exactly d'you mean, any road – canoodling?'

'Well . . . He was kissing her.'

'No harm in that, Jack. A kiss in a car!'

'Pat wouldn't like it. She told me last night, while we waited for Sandie to get in – she's never even met the lad.'

'You didn't tell Pat about this?'

'No fear. She were upset enough when half-ten came and no Sandie.'

'But the lass weren't very late? I think I heard her come in – about eleven.'

'Eleven o'clock's late for a lass who knows the curfew is ten o'clock.'

'What did you expect?' Matt murmured. 'She was bound to stay out to show you you couldn't order her around.'

'I didn't order. I offered to take her home.'

'Still . . .'

'If it was a daughter of yours, you'd have said nothing?' Jack challenged.

Matt paused with the water-hose in his hand. 'I'd have said hullo. Happen I'd have asked to be introduced. I wouldn't have got their backs up. Kids have their pride!'

Jack made no reply. Matt turned on the water and began

to hose down. Jack hung up his white coat and stood watching him, hands in pockets. He wondered now what the proper course of action would have been. Being father to a grown family wasn't as easy as he had imagined.

Matt looked up. 'Sithee, Jack . . . The most important thing is, she's not your daughter –'

'But I –'

'You feel in place of a father. All right. But you're a *stepfather*. By all accounts, it's a difficult part to play. You only have to remember the fairy tales about wicked stepmothers to see how hard it is to get a good relationship with stepchildren.'

'You think I made a mistake.'

'It ain't what I think, Jack. It's Sandie. And I bet she feels you were just being interfering.'

'Oh, thanks a million.'

Dolly put her head round the door of the mistle to say breakfast was ready.

'Is Jackie up and off to work?' Jack enquired.

'Finally. That makes at least some slight space round the breakfast table.'

Jack frowned, and looked as if he were about to say the boy had a perfect right to a place at table. Instead he said, 'Oh, well, once he's used to the routine, he'll stir his stumps earlier. I've told him to be careful when he gets up, not to rouse Grandad if he's sleeping.'

'Grandad's not worried about waking up in the morning,' Dolly remarked. 'It's Jackie who's doing the complaining.' She shrugged slightly and went out.

Jack watched her disappear from view. 'She's a bit tetchy with me these days,' he observed. 'I'm sorry she's upset over the barn conversion, Matt, but I'm sure you do see –'

'We don't want to go over that, Jack. It was settled at the meeting.'

'I just wish Dolly could take it in that spirit.'

At this implied criticism of his wife, Matt came to the end of his patience. 'You're no help, are you, when you start telling us what great plans you've got for the place!'

'Well, I can't just act as if I wasn't going to do anything –'

'No one's asking you to. But Dolly can't help her feelings, and you ought to understand the whole thing's been a bitter disappointment to her.'

It had never occurred to Jack that Dolly had been so serious about her plan. He had taken it for granted that he and she had both had the same good idea, at about the same level of earnestness. He had no idea of the dreams she'd invested in her scheme of a home for herself and Matt and her baby.

'I understand she's disappointed –'

'She's stricken – that's the word for it.'

'There's no sense in dramatizing –'

Matt stalked to the faucet, turned off the water, and threw down the hose. 'You coil that up and stow it away,' he commanded. 'It's a better way to use your time than standing here talking rubbish!'

With which, he walked out.

Jack stared after him in bewilderment. He had never heard Matt lose his temper before. It was as if the roof had fallen in on him.

Chapter Four

Matt was right when he said Sandie would resent Jack's interference. When Pat began a scolding about staying out so late, particularly when next day was a school day, Sandie came right back with her complaint.

'Teddy's all right, Mum, he's no different from any other boy. I'd have got him to run me home by quarter to eleven at the latest, if Jack hadn't interfered!'

'Jack?' Pat said in amazement, turning from the bedmaking in Jackie's little room.

'Aye, he drove up and slammed on the brakes when he saw me and Teddy parked in Teddy's car near the Woolpack –'

'Oh, Sandie!'

'Don't say it in that tone of voice. We weren't doing anything, just having a drink.'

'A drink!'

'It wasn't anything, Mum. Teddy had lager, I had a shandy but I didn't drink much, I didn't fancy it –'

'He'd no right to buy you shandy.'

'Oh, Mum! Lots of girls drink it. It's not alcoholic.'

'It certainly is! It's got beer or lager in it.'

'That's why it tastes so funny, I suppose. Look, that's not what I want to talk about. Jack had no right to be giving me orders.'

'What orders did he give you? If he told you to stop drinking shandy out of a can in a boy's car –'

'He'd no *right*! That's what I'm trying to tell you, Mum. He's not my Dad. I'm not Jackie!'

As soon as she'd said it, she was sorry, and when she saw her mother flinch she half put out a hand. 'That wasn't very nice, Sandie,' Pat said in a muffled voice, spreading the counterpane smooth.

'*He* wasn't very nice to me and Teddy.' To cover her sense of shame, the girl began stuffing schoolbooks in her satchel. She hated to hurt her mother. She felt she'd suffered enough in the past without having little niggling anxieties now. But she couldn't get over her sense of injured pride at Jack's behaviour.

'Well, let's forget about last night, love. Why don't you bring Teddy to tea on Saturday?'

'Oh no!'

'But why not?'

'You think I want him here, being given the once over to see if he's a suitable companion for me?'

'It won't be like that, Sandie.'

'Then why d'you want me to invite him?'

Pat sighed. 'Is it so very strange when I want to meet my daughter's friends?'

Feeling somehow she was now in the wrong, Sandie flounced past her to the door. 'I'll invite Betty Oates, then,' she said in a pert voice, 'she's a friend!'

Later in the morning, Pat sought out Jack where he was finishing a chat with the architect in the old barn. He introduced her, there was a little conversation about getting the application for planning permission off that very day, the architect shook hands and left. 'He's keen,' Jack observed with satisfaction. 'Says he likes a challenge like this and he'll draw up some interesting plans.'

Pat turned her tawny head to gaze about her at the place. 'Won't it cost a pretty penny, having an architect and all that? They don't work for nowt, do they?'

'It's worth it – can't botch a job like this, can't have modern rubbish tacked in here and there just because it's cheap. We've got to have proper windowframes to match the building, and all that.' He paused. 'Don't mention it to Dolly, though, will you? I gather she's a bit touchy on the subject.'

'She's not the only one who's touchy,' Pat remarked. 'What happened with you and Sandie last night?'

Jack raised his brows. 'Oh, she told you, did she?'

'Did you expect her not to?'

He hesitated. 'I was wondering whether to mention it. I didn't want to get her into trouble – seems like tale-telling – but it was a bit much.'

'She's very upset about it,' she said.

'Upset?' He recalled Matt's opinion on the subject. 'Oh . . . Well, I'm sorry, of course, but the fellow seemed a bit of a tearaway – and they were sitting there with the car lights switched off.'

Since he hadn't mentioned it, Pat didn't bring up the matter of the cans of drink. 'She says you were bossy.'

'Bossy? Well, I suggested strongly that she should get off home. It was after ten, you know. And we don't want her getting in trouble, do we?'

At that word, Pat's opinion, until then inclined towards Jack, veered towards Sandie. Jack seemed unaware of what it meant to her. 'Listen, Jack, she told me very pointedly that you had no right, that you aren't *her* father.'

'I didn't – ' he broke off. 'Oh, I see.' He was brought up short by the revelation that Sandie had no intention of accepting him as a parent, whatever his true relationship with her brother. It shocked him. Until then he'd taken it for granted that Sandie liked him and would be glad of his guidance. Jackie, he knew, had taken an unreasoning dislike to him but Sandie he had always thought of as a young friend. To discover she resented his guardianship was like a slap in the face.

Matt put his head round the barn door. 'You ready to go

into Hotten? We really need that di-methoate if I'm going to do the spraying.'

His voice almost died away. The tension in the air between Pat and Jack twanged like a bow-string. He made himself scarce at once.

Annie appeared at the house door. 'Matt!' she called. 'You're wanted on the phone!'

He crossed the farmyard and went indoors, hoping it would be Millers saying they'd got a delivery of insecticide. When he announced himself, he was astonished to find himself being addressed by Alan Turner of N.Y. Estates.

'Ah, Matt,' said Turner grandly. 'Glad to get hold of you. Listen, Joe's been telling me you're interested in Tolly Farmhouse?'

'Eh?' Matt said in disbelief.

'He was wrong then?'

'Nay, nay, he were right!'

'Well, that's good, I'm glad I had the right end of the stick. Listen, I don't know for sure . . . Would it be a good idea for us to meet and talk about it?'

'Talk about it? Well, of course, I'm only too –'

'How about bringing Mrs Skilbeck up here one evening, eh? Just for a drink and a chat. Are you free tonight?'

'We-ell . . . Not tonight.' Matt's instinct was to allow time to think about this sudden intervention from outside.

'I can't do tomorrow night – got an engagement in Connelton. How about . . . day after tomorrow . . . Say about eightish?'

'Yes . . . yes . . . that would be fine.'

'Righto then. Look forward.'

Matt replaced the phone with a thunderstruck look on his face. Luckily he was facing the dresser, away from Annie, who was mixing a cake at the kitchen table. 'Had some luck about the chemicals?' she enquired, having half heard his end of the conversation.

'Nay, Jack's just going to drive into Hotten to see if he can track some down.' Matt went out, thus avoiding having to say what he'd been talking about. He was still too overcome to be able to discuss it. That Turner should approach him was amazing. To have to tell Annie they might be on the point of moving out to a house on N.Y.

property was just one thing too many.

Alan Turner replaced the phone feeling very pleased with himself. He had heard the astonishment in Matt's voice but he had also heard something else, something very important – dawning gratitude. He went to the door of the study and called: 'Joe?'

'Yes?' Joe called back from his office down the passage.

'Can you spare a moment?'

Joe appeared, a clipboard with work schedules in his hand. 'If it's about the spraying –'

'Oh, don't worry about that. I've sorted that out. We should be getting a delivery tomorrow morning some time. Have Hooson and young Merrick standing by to unload, eh? Don't want to delay the truck – it's not exactly an unscheduled stop but the driver's putting himself out to help us.'

Joe privately awarded full marks to Turner. There was no way he himself could have conjured up di-methoate from nowhere. 'Will do,' he confirmed.

'Have you seen this report from HQ?' Turner was offering him a one page note.

Joe cast his eye over it. Subsidy opportunities . . . winter feed allowance . . . unsuitable for cattle but sheep grazing . . .

'I've always said we could run at least another hundred up over the Struggle,' he remarked. 'Glad they see it my way.'

'Yes, it's one up to you. Let's hope they give you credit for your conclusions.'

'I'd rather have a rise,' he joked.

'Now, now, you know I told you your salary review isn't due yet.' But Turner knew he wasn't serious. 'Will you keep an eye on the market and let me know when's the best time to buy the new flock? Then we'll get moving.'

'Hey-up,' Joe protested. 'Jesse Gillan is getting on. He'll be retiring inside a twelvemonth. He's not going to agree to being loaded with an extra hundred sheep.' He paused, thinking of Jesse's calm, adamant features. 'In fact, he'll refuse to take them on. He wouldn't want to have more sheep than he could see after.'

Turner threw himself into his office chair, stretched out

his legs in their dogtooth slacks, and regarded his suede chukka boots with satisfaction. 'I've been thinking about that. With Jesse's retirement looming, it's as well to start looking for a replacement. We'd want him to work his way in, learn the ropes of N.Y.'s methods. And we'd want a good man.'

'Not so easy, Alan. Good shepherds aren't standing around waiting to be hired like tractor hands.'

'No, and to tell you the truth, Head Office didn't like the way your friend Jesse took a beating at the last show.'

'Oh, come on, you can't call it that! He just didn't have the right beasts at the right time.'

'But "face" is important to N.Y. If they enter a show, they like to win, or at least come in the first three. They don't want a no-place result.' He paused, enjoying the surprise he was going to spring. 'Who's the best man around here?'

'Matt Skilbeck,' Joe returned without hesitation. 'But there's no hope of getting him.'

'You don't think it's even worth trying?'

'He'd no more think of leaving Emmerdale than flying to the moon,' Joe said with total certainty.

Turner took a moment before he went on. Joe's tone had suddenly reminded him that these two men, Joe and Matt, had once worked alongside each other, were very close. 'Just a minute,' he said. 'You're a director of Emmerdale Farm, of course.'

'Well, that's no secret.'

'So of course it's in your interest on that score to keep Matt Skilbeck there.'

'It's nowt to do with –'

'Which hat are you wearing at the moment, Joe, when you talk about Matt never leaving Emmerdale?'

'It's not a question of hats,' Joe said, uncomfortably. 'I know Matt. He'd never leave Emmerdale. It's his life, that's all.'

Turner smiled. 'But he needs somewhere to live, doesn't he? And we can offer him that.'

'Tolly Farmhouse?' Joe said, catching on. 'You'd make a condition?'

'This is a confidential business matter. You're wearing

56

your N.Y. Estates hat now, remember that. I'm going to offer Matt Skilbeck Tolly's as a tied cottage to go with the job of shepherd.'

Joe was dumbfounded. It was so neat, so tricky! He himself had offered this chance to Turner on a plate by suggesting the farmhouse should be offered to rent. Dolt that he was! Why hadn't he foreseen that Turner would use it to his own advantage? For it would be to his advantage, there was no doubt about it. To take on a hundred extra sheep on land that was going more or less to waste at present, to hire the best shepherd in the district, to do well with the flock and probably win those prestigious prizes at the shows . . . It was a beautiful piece of strategy.

And moreover, there was no doubt Turner would get enjoyment out of it. He'd be taking Matt away from Jack Sugden, his chief enemy in the area. He'd be doing something for Matt that Jack Sugden couldn't do, giving him a house and a good salary and scope to work as he liked. He'd be able to point to his actions and say: 'The man was wasted at Emmerdale. But it took *me* to see it.'

In that he was wrong. Joe had always understood and appreciated Matt's worth. It was only that, placed as they were at Emmerdale, they'd never had the funds to give Matt his chance with the sheep. He recalled with bitter amusement the fight Matt had had to get a mere seven hundred pounds invested in some lambing shelter. Jack had wanted to throw the money away on some scheme of his own. But if Matt came to N.Y., he'd have funds at his disposal to run the sheep in whatever way he chose, so long as it was within the dictates of good business.

'Is it understood, then, Joe?' Turner demanded. 'You say nothing of all this to anyone?'

Joe nodded. He knew he was honour-bound, as an employee of N.Y. Estates, to do nothing that would jeopardize their interests.

When he went to the Woolpack that lunchtime for a pint, he decided he'd try to drop a hint to Henry. Henry was quick on the uptake, didn't need to have everything spelt out to him. Henry gave him the opportunity by remarking: 'Architect dropped in here for a ploughman's before he went back to Harrogate. Been taking a dekko at

Jack's barn.'

'Oh aye,' said Joe. 'What d'you reckon?

'He didn't say much. Just enthused a bit over what a lovely old building it is – and I suppose it *is*, if you stop to think on it. Sturdy as Cummin Crag, is yon.'

'Aye. I've been thinking, Henry . . .'

'Well, what?' Henry said as Joe hesitated how to choose his words.

'Happen we were a bit hasty over voting to let Jack have it.'

Henry recalled the meeting. 'He was first in with the idea.'

'I daresay. But Dolly and Matt had had their eye on it for a long time.'

'Had either of them told you that?'

'Not exactly. But Matt said –'

'I got the impression they were just thinking it over. If they'd been set on it, surely they'd have said summat earlier?'

'But on the other hand –'

'How do we know,' Henry went on, disregarding the beginning of Joe's argument, 'that Jack and Pat hadn't been thinking about it a long time before the idea jelled?'

Oh, get on with you, Joe said internally, can't you see I'm trying to *tell* you something? Aloud he said, 'I just feel the company ought to find Matt somewhere of his own to live. He's been with us a long time now, seems only grateful to do summat, for with the baby coming . . . things won't be easy for them, will they?'

'I always understood that attic room was very nice – more like a . . . what do they call it . . . a studio flat than a bedsit.'

'Happen. But how d'you like to do a hard day's work and then sleep in the same room wi' a fretful baby?'

'Um,' said Henry, much struck. 'Do you mean buy them something? That'd cost a fortune.'

This was only too true, and Joe knew as well as anyone that they couldn't afford to do that. Not too long ago they'd had to make a choice over spending money on Matt's sheep-housing or Hathersage land, and had chosen in favour of Matt. To keep Jack happy, Henry himself had advanced the money for Jack to take Hathersage out of the Emmerdale rota of crop production and try it as an organic unit. Where could the money come from to buy a house for Matt? Certainly not from the bank, which was already beginning to make anxious noises as the depression bit at its resources.

What he wanted was for Matt and Dolly to get the converted barn. That was the easy solution and, to his mind, only fair. You might say that Jack, newly married, ought to be so pleased with his lot that he didn't want anything else! He ought to be ready to give up the barn to Matt. But how to convey this message?

'One day Jack'll inherit the farmhouse, won't he?' he suggested. 'Only right, eldest son . . . And he'll be expected to live there, don't you reckon?'

Henry thought that was looking very far ahead. Annie was not likely to quit this vale of tears for many a year. All the same he sensed a hint in this somewhere. 'Are you suggesting we tell Jack the house is his domain and he ought to let Matt and Dolly have the barn?'

'More or less.'

Amos appeared. It was close to lunchtime closing. 'Now then, gents,' he warned.

Henry frowned at him so intensely that he almost withdrew. But Henry's frown was for what Joe had just said. 'Have you mentioned this to anyone else?' Joe shook his head. 'Not to Annie?'

'I thought it best to see how you felt first.'

'I dunno what to say,' Henry confessed, blowing out a breath. 'It's out o' the blue. I mean, changing our opinion at this late stage. I hate to think what Jack would say – or more important, Pat.'

Amos, having shooed out a couple of tardy customers, came back to the pair so deep in conversation. 'Now then, Joe! Mr Wilks! I look to you to set an example. I've been calling drink up.'

'All right, Amos, I'm going,' Joe said. He drained the dregs of his pint. To Henry he said, 'Think over what I said, will you?'

Henry nodded, an air of mystification on his face as he watched him walk out. What could be the reason for this change of face from Joe? Joe had not argued when Matt gave in over the allotting of the barn at the meeting. Mind you . . . now he thought of it . . . Joe had really not been in favour. But Henry had put that down, perhaps mistakenly, to one more example of the resentment that seemed to simmer between these two.

No doubt about it, Joe had reason to be irritated with Jack. Jack's stubborn views about farming, his dislike of what he termed 'agro-business', brought him into conflict very often with Joe's employers. That must make life difficult for the younger brother.

And then Joe was a good farmer. Modern, though not carried away by every new fad of mechanization or chemicals. Level-headed about business – while in his hands Emmerdale had always shown a profit. How it must annoy him to see Jack turning from one scheme to another, getting them deeper into debt to finance his plans, and neglecting the day-to-day work while he attended to Hathersage. Then all this business over Pat Merrick – Pat Sugden as she now was. Of course Jack and Pat were entitled to their happiness just like everyone else, but Lord! – what a public show they had made of themselves.

Henry, serving in the Woolpack every day with Amos, heard what the villagers said about such things. The Beckindalers were not unkind folk, but they were inclined to feel amusement and a faint contempt for Jack's behaviour. Joe must be aware of this, even though he didn't hear as much of it as Henry did. It must irk him to know that Emmerdale, once admired as a farm that paid its way, improved its land, and won prizes for its ewes at county shows, was now chiefly famous for being in the hands of the eccentric Jack Sugden, one-time bestselling novelist, ladies' man and marriage-wrecker. For Beckindale believed, almost to a man, that Pat would never have divorced Tom Merrick if Jack Sugden hadn't talked her into it.

This business of the barn, though . . . Was Joe now saying Matt ought to have it just to deprive Jack of it? No, no. Joe wasn't ungenerous. More likely he simply felt an injustice had been done.

Was he right? Ought Henry to have gone into the case

more thoroughly at the meeting? Yet Annie had wanted Jack to have it, and Henry was always very influenced by what Annie wanted. He wished her to be happy. It was one of his chief aims in life. All the same . . . Would Annie really be happy to see Matt suffer an injustice?

The same thought was occupying Sam Pearson. Sam, having long ago sold out his share in Emmerdale to Henry, had no voting rights and wasn't allowed to attend board meetings. He had had to learn the news of the barn conversion from his daughter Annie when that fateful meeting broke up. 'Thee gave it to Jack?' he said in surprise. 'But Jack ought to live in t'house! He's farming Emmerdale land, isn't he? He ought to live in Emmerdale farmhouse.'

'Well, now, Dad,' Annie said, 'Joe farmed Emmerdale, but lived at Demdyke the while.'

'That were different,' Sam said in a low voice. 'He were living wi' that Kathy Gimbel at the time. You couldn't have had him here, carrying on wi' a lass outside the bounds of wedlock. What I'm talking about now,' and he spoke out with conviction, 'is that the head of the farm is the head of the house.'

Annie smiled. 'I don't want to argue, Dad, but in Jacob's will it stated plainly that the house was to be mine as long as I lived.'

'Oh, that,' her father said with scorn. 'That's not what I'm talking about. Farmer should live in farmer's house. That's sense.'

But his view had carried no weight, and he'd mentioned it only to Annie.

Today, as it happened, he found Matt in his shed looking for a wrench to deal with a difficult screw on the baler. 'I thought you were hay-making?'

'We are, Dad, but we've been a bit put out of schedule by that architect taking Jack away for an hour and now Jack's gone off to Hotten on the track of di-methoate.' He found the wrench he wanted behind a piece of sacking. 'All right if I borrow?'

'If you put it back in its right place.' Matt smothered a grin at the thought of the right place being under an old

61

sack. 'This architect feller . . . He'll do t'barn up to Jack's specification, will he?'

'I s'pose so.'

'You should have had that barn, Matt.'

Matt straightened, looking at him in surprise.

'Aye, you should,' the old man went on, concern on his freckled face. 'You and Dolly are entitled to a place of your own.'

'We'll get one, eventually.'

'I can't see how, wi' prices the way they are round here. All those incomers,' Sam mourned, 'taking up the places for holiday letting –'

'It brings money into the district, Grandad –'

'Only in summer. They lie empty all winter and get damp and diseased wi' dry rot . . . If they'd even rent 'em out in the winter, but they won't, not if there's a chance under this funny law of somebody acquiring the right to stay. And they charge the earth if they do take tenants.'

Matt could see the old man was genuinely distressed about it. 'There's a chance, though,' he murmured. 'N.Y.'s got a spare house and –'

'A cottage from N.Y. Estates?'

'Tolly Farmhouse, you know. And it's next to our land, right handy.' Matt fiddled with the ratchet of the wrench. 'Seems a bit loose, this, Grandad. Will it move a tight screw?'

'Move anything, that will,' Sam said. Then, as Matt began to turn away, 'Matt . . . Not thinking of working for N.Y., are you?'

Matt laughed. 'Come off it, Grandad! How'd you manage without me?' Still chuckling, he went out. Sam shrugged and went back to the piece of wood he was turning for a carving.

Next morning at eleven the promised di-methoate was duly delivered at Home Farm. Jackie Merrick and Teddy Hooson manhandled the small drums down off the truck and stacked them outside the store-shed. It was hot work so before they began to shift them inside after the truck's departure, they paused for a drink. Teddy had a flask of tea. They sat inside the store-room, on the stacked sacks of seed-dressing.

Teddy related his encounter with Jack Sugden, knowing it would interest Jackie to have yet another example of his stepfather's unreasonableness. Jackie didn't take it with quite as much enthusiasm as he expected.

'Mum was right put out about it,' he told the other boy. 'You've got to understand, Mum's very protective towards Sandie.'

'She won't stop her coming out though, will she?'

Jackie shrugged.

'What's that mean?' Teddy insisted.

'It means I dunno. Depends how Jack Sugden painted it to her.'

Teddy cleared his throat and spat expressively. 'Needs his nose rubbing in summat, if you ask me!'

Whatever Jackie might have replied was lost in the arrival of Joe Sugden, not looking best pleased. 'It's okay to have a tea-break, but not a morning off,' he remarked at sight of their lolling attitude. He pointed to the plastic kegs of chemical. 'I want them inside by twelve so get cracking.'

'We've not stopped ten minutes,' Jackie told him with entire honesty.

'Huh,' Joe said, which meant he might believe it or he might not. 'I'll be back in half an hour and I don't want to see those drums outside. That's expensive stuff, understand?'

'Yes, sir; no, sir,' Teddy said when the boss was safely out of hearing. 'He's a slave driver, isn't he?'

'He ain't bad,' Jackie said. 'Works hard himself, expects the same from the rest.'

'Well, you could have fooled me – he was complaining afore he even saw us.'

'Must be summat up. He's not usually so bad.'

Teddy began to laugh as he screwed the cap back on his flask. 'Perhaps his brother caught *him* out late!'

Jackie smiled. 'Could be. There's no love lost atween them.'

'Why not?' Teddy said, ever eager for information that might prove useful.

'Dunno.' Jackie went outside and began to heft the little

kegs indoors. 'They just don't seem to get on. Jack's into this natural farming kick, so he don't like this farm.'

'What farm? Oh, you mean N.Y.?'

'That's right. Thinks it's immoral or something, to make a profit. And wi' his brother working here, they've got a bone of contention between 'em all the time. I s'pose that's the reason.'

They worked for a while in silence. Teddy's thoughts, fixed on the insult he'd suffered at the hands of Jack Sugden, led him to ask: 'Will you go on living at Emmerdale wi' your Mum and Dad now they're married?' As Jackie whirled on him in anger he said quickly, 'No offence. It just came out like that.'

'I don't think of him as my Dad,' Jackie said in a hard voice. He dumped kegs about with emphasis.

'Can't say I blame you,' Teddy agreed. 'But I mean, you used to live in that caravan where I met Sandie . . . You going to live at Emmerdale now?'

'Why?'

'Well, he'll really have his eye on you, won't he? Be like living wi' your schoolteacher!'

Jackie kept his attention on his work. But the words sank deep into him. It was a dreadful prospect.

At midday Joe arrived to check over what they had done and send Jackie back to work with the gamekeeper Seth Armstrong. His mood seemed a little lightened from what it had been. 'Well, you'll be spraying this afternoon,' he said to Teddy.

'It's what I should be doing,' Teddy agreed, but meaning he thought hefting drums of chemical was below his status.

'You understand about the mixing?' Joe asked. 'The proportions?'

'It's all here,' Teddy said, showing the bright label affixed to each drum.

'Aye, looks right,' Joe said, studying the drum nearest him.

'Ought to be, didn't it?' Teddy said in a flip tone.

Joe gave him a glance.

'I mean, they make it – if they don't get it right, who does?' Teddy back-pedalled rather hastily. He ought to remember to be a bit careful with Joe Sugden. He wasn't as soft a touch as Alan Turner.

'You see you stick to the letter of the rules,' Joe said. 'Do you know where the water feed is?'

'Round the corner, isn't it?' For a moment Teddy considered throwing in 'sir'.

'Aye, but watch it. The tap's liable to gushing.'

'I'll see it just fills the tank.'

'Just warning you against a drenching,' Joe said in a peaceable tone, to show that he could be kindhearted when he got a decent tone in return. But he didn't really take to Teddy Hooson very much.

He had moved further into the storehouse, his eye caught by a big plastic bottle. 'What's that doing here?' he demanded of no one in particular.

'It was here when we moved in the di-meth, Mr Sugden.'

'Well, it shouldn't be.' Joe picked up first one bottle and then another, stacking them well away in a corner. 'Don't do to get these things mixed up.'

'Hardly likely. They're different shapes.'

'Better safe than sorry,' Joe said, and put the four big demi-john sized bottles by themselves with a space between them and the di-methoate. 'I think it was left over when we sprayed the thistles in March. Just steer clear, eh?'

'Righto, Mr Sugden.' Interfering git, he added to himself as Joe went briskly away.

Joe's mood had somewhat improved because, having thought over the problem of losing Matt to N.Y.'s employment, he felt he might hope for some move by Henry. He hadn't been able to come out in the open and say: 'Do something!' but he felt that Henry, quick as he was, must have guessed what he was on about.

It was therefore something of a slap in the face to find Alan Turner looking smug and giving instructions to Pat Merrick about tidying up the study. 'I'm having people in for drinks, you see,' he told her. 'Want to make a good impression and to be honest it's a bit of a mess in here.'

'I can put away a lot of the paper, Mr Turner,' Pat agreed. 'It needs filing, in any case.'

'You're such a help, Pat! What would we do in the office without you?' He paused, looking at her, but Pat let the opening go by. 'You will be staying on?' Alan enquired.

'What? Oh . . . yes . . . why not?'

'I thought . . . your husband . . . He and I don't see eye to eye. I thought he might object to your working for N.Y.'

'Oh, there's no question of that,' Pat said blithely.

'Good. I shouldn't like to have to start looking for a new clerk.'

'Then if that's all right, Mr Turner, can I leave now for my lunch break? Mrs Sugden's expecting me back for the meal.'

'I'll run you home, Pat,' Joe offered.

'Nay, Jack's collecting me at Verney lane-end,' she said, with a little smile of thanks.

When she'd gone, Alan picked up the mug of coffee she'd made when she broke off typing. He sipped thoughtfully. 'You want me, Joe?' he asked.

'Did you want to look at that new silage container they're putting up at Porford? Because ours at Ridge Farm'll need replacing soon and I thought you'd like to take a dekko.'

'Oh, that's today, is it? I've a note of it somewhere.' He ferreted around among a pile of paper. 'Yes. I told Mr Blackett I'd drop by so I'd best be off. I'll get a bite to eat and then go straight on there.'

'Okay.'

'I won't come back till tomorrow. It's not worth making the journey both ways in one day.'

'Back in the morning, then?'

'Yes, and if I'm late, Joe . . . You heard me asking Pat to tidy up a bit . . . see she does it.'

Joe said nothing. He knew Pat well enough to believe she'd do what she said she'd do.

'I'm having Matt and Dolly round for drinks, you see,' said Alan.

'Alan; listen –'

'Don't say it, Joe,' said Turner, holding up a hand. 'We want the best shepherd we can find. If that's Matt Skilbeck, then it's him I'm going after.'

'I can understand that, Alan,' Joe said. 'But it's not easy for me.'

Alan smiled without sincerity. 'That's your bother, I'm afraid, Joe. I sympathize, but I can't take notice of it. N.Y.

pay my salary and yours. Unless you want to leave N.Y. – is that it?'

Joe felt a great desire to hit him. His job was being threatened if he didn't toe the line, over a matter where he already knew his ethical obligation was to his employer. He curbed his temper and began, 'It's only –'

'There's no room for "it's only" in business. I'm doing what I can for you – I'm handling the approach to Skilbeck myself so you won't be directly involved in divided loyalties. All you have to do,' Turner said in a tone of sympathetic generosity that rang absolutely false, 'is keep your mouth shut.'

Chapter Five

Despite Turner's warning, Joe felt honour-bound to do something about Matt leaving Emmerdale. He dropped in at late morning, when he knew from experience that his mother was generally alone.

'Hello!' she cried when he walked in. Visits from Joe were rare these days. 'Come for coffee?'

'Nay, I were on my way to look at some drainage work up t'Struggle. How's things?'

'Oh, fine, fine . . .' Yet she didn't look exactly convinced as she said it. He thought to himself, Say what you like, coping with such a full house is no joke. Cooking every day for eight people, and one of them a healthy boy with an enormous appetite . . .

'How's Grandad?'

'Surprisingly happy. He's taken to young Jackie.'

'Good for him.'

'Oh, give Grandad a bit of time and he's good-natured enough to live with anybody.'

Joe didn't altogether agree with this. He'd had many a bad time with his grandfather. But he hadn't come to argue. 'It must still be a big change for him, sharing his room wi' a youngster.'

'Aye, but it won't be for long. Jack's saying now, the architect feels the barn can be ready in about eight weeks.'

He raised his eyebrows. Eight weeks? Not likely. Still . . . 'I've been thinking, Ma . . . Happen we made a mistake letting Pat and Jack have the barn.'

Annie paused in her task. She was shelling peas for the midday meal. She looked up.

'See, Jack's going to inherit the house one day, isn't he?' Joe plodded on. 'It seems kind of wrong for him to be living elsewhere and then move back some day.'

She smiled. 'I'm not thinking of leaving the place vacant for a while yet, love.'

'Nay, I'm not thinking along those lines. I'm thinking about the rightness of it. Is it fair, I mean – when in fact Jack will own the house, to let him own the barn too?'

Annie's smile faded. 'The barn belongs to the company,' she said.

'We know that, Ma,' he replied impatiently. 'That's the point! I've told Henry, so I may as well tell you. I think we ought to have let Matt and Dolly have the barn. Jack and Pat ought to live here with you. That's the tradition and I don't see why it should be changed in Jack's favour.'

Annie didn't reply for a moment. Her hands became automatically busy with the peas. At last she said : 'You didn't say anything at the meeting.'

'It was all a bit of a surprise. I didn't have time to think about it properly.'

'Have you said owt to Jack?'

He shook his head with vehemence. They both knew that anything sounding the least like criticism from Joe would send Jack into stubborn opposition. 'I thought it'd sound better coming from you.'

'But . . . it would seem so odd. He's got the plans out, he's getting planning permission . . .'

At this crucial moment the phone rang. Joe, gesturing to his mother not to disturb herself, went to answer. He turned with the receiver held out. 'It's Henry. He wants a word.'

He knew, as he spoke, that Henry had rung to speak about his hint over the barn. Annie took the phone and said hello. On the other end Henry said, 'So Joe's there, is he? He been talking about Jack and the barn?'

'Aye, Henry, as a matter of fact –'

'He's been chatting to me. It took me aback.'

'Me too, lad.'

'Listen, don't let on to him, but I think there's more to it than meets the eye. It's got me a bit bothered. Best not say owt while he's with you. I'll drop by later and have a talk. Will you be in this afternoon?'

'I can make sure I am.'

'Righto, see you then.'

She hung up. Joe was standing halfway to the door, watching her. She said, 'He's coming round this afternoon for a chat.'

'Good,' Joe said, and walked out without more ado.

He's worried, she thought. Whatever can be the matter?

Henry arrived as soon as he thought she would have cleared up after the midday meal. He was his usual spruce self in a pair of whipcords and a light check jacket. He accepted with alacrity Annie's offer of a cup of tea and a piece of parkin, today having been Amos's turn to cook the lunch; it had consisted of a rather meagre lamb chop, potatoes, and a piece of shop-bought treacle tart which he'd had to give up after the first mouthful because it was so cardboardy.

'Na' then,' he said after the first appreciative crunch, 'what's Joe been saying?'

She recounted the conversation, her tone dubious. Henry sat nodding. 'He said almost the same thing to me. Funny, isn't it?'

She refilled his cup as she replied. 'What's funnier is that it's right – in principle, I mean. Jack *will* get the farmhouse because he's running the farm and it's the obvious place for the farmer to live . . .'

'But strictly speaking, Annie, there's no reason why Matt shouldn't get it. The house is owned by Emmerdale Farm Limited: we can allot it to whoever we please, and Matt has an equal share.'

'But he don't run the farm and he's never likely to – he wouldn't if you asked him. He'd say that it's Jack's job and he's just the worker.'

Henry was rubbing his chin in thought. 'What I don't understand is, what difference does it make? The barn is just across the yard from the house. What difference does it make who lives where? What's the point of Joe's argument?'

'I take it,' she said, picking her words, 'Joe's come to think Matt and Dolly have been hard done by.'

'I sympathize wi' that view myself, having had time to stand back and review it. If Jack hadn't got in first, there's no doubt but that Matt would have got the barn. But we can't take it off Jack *now*.'

'What I've been thinking is . . . You know Joe's never agreed with how Jack runs the farm. Happen he's thinking that if Matt and Dolly get a place even a bit away, it'll leave Jack that bit more free to . . . to . . .'

'You don't want Matt and Dolly too far away either, do you?' he enquired sympathetically.

'I'd miss Dolly very much. She's a lovely lass to have about the place.'

'Aye,' he agreed. 'Happen we rely too much on her good nature, and Matt's too.'

They came to no useful conclusion. Their view was that what's done is done and Jack must have the barn.

Joe, unaware that his moves had accomplished nothing, was going about the day's work in a more optimistic frame of mind. He drove about the estate casting an eye on what was being done and what needed to be planned next. He was therefore surprised to see no sign of Teddy Hooson in the field where he was supposed to be working. The tractor and sprayer were there, unattended, but the lad was absent.

He drove on after a momentary pause. Drinking his flask of tea behind some hedge, probably.

At the crossroads he saw the Emmerdale Land-Rover approaching from the Hotten road. He drew up. Jack did likewise then came over to speak to him. 'I'm sick of traipsing round looking for di-methoate, Joe. Would it be asking too much to borrow some from you? Our delivery's late.'

'There's been a strike at the depot,' Joe explained. 'We had trouble too.'

'Oh, no luck then?'

70

It didn't occur to Joe to refuse. This was not a personal thing, it was a matter of good farming. Now was the time to spray against potato blight and other diseases, and Emmerdale's crops needed protection just as much as N.Y. Estates'. In fact, it pleased him that Jack was actually considering a chemical product without argument.

'I reckon we can manage a bit. Follow me up to Home Farm.'

At the stores Joe unlocked and shifted a couple of drums towards the door. 'There you are. Pay us back when you eventually get delivery.'

'What I'd like to know,' Jack said with envy, 'is how you managed to get it when we couldn't?'

'Ah, when you're Alan Turner, all things are possible.'

'Got a load of Páraquat too, I see – was that just delivered?'

'Nay, that's from March. Now don't start giving me a lecture on the evils of all-purpose weedkillers. They're necessary in the way we run the farms and that's an end of it.'

Jack shook his head. 'If you sprayed that load on the fields, it'd be pretty near the end of everything growing around here!'

'No danger,' Joe said easily. 'Here, grab this.' He rolled the keg towards Jack and as they put the two in the Emmerdale vehicle he changed the subject to the barn conversion.

'We're waiting for planning permission,' Jack told him. 'Next meeting of the Council's next week and the architect says he thinks it'll go through on the nod, but there's nowt we can do until then.'

Joe said cautiously: 'I'm surprised you want to go there. I'd have thought you'd want to live in the old home.'

'I like the idea of the barn. So does Pat.'

'But you'll inherit the house. Bound to, as the eldest.'

'It don't follow that we'd want to live in it. Matt and Dolly can have it.'

'But they're looking for somewhere else. Once they move out, they might not want to move back.'

'Then you can have it,' Jack said lightly. 'Who knows, you might get married again.'

Joe said with an earnest undertone, 'But it'd mean a lot to Ma and Grandad to think of you in the old house. I reckon they'd like to know the Sugdens would still be living and farming there after they've gone.'

'Getting a bit morbid, aren't you?' his brother said, eyeing him. 'Ma's good for another twenty years, and I daresay Grandad too!' He climbed into the Land-Rover.

'But if Matt and Dolly move away – as far as Hotten, mebbe – and you're in the barn, Ma and Grandad will be alone in the house.'

'We'll be next door, it's hardly a worry, is it?'

'But Ma'll miss Dolly and Matt.'

That was true, and had not occurred to Jack. But he had his answer in a moment. 'You could give 'em Demdyke, couldn't you? Then they'd only be a few minutes away in Beckindale. Think about that, little brother!'

He grinned and nodded, started the engine, and drove off briskly. Joe stood looking after him with his dark face creased in exasperation.

Jack, driving through Beckindale a moment later on his way home, was a little taken aback to see his stepdaughter Sandie at the bus stop, having clearly just alighted. She was deep in conversation with Teddy Hooson, who was sitting in his gaudy car a few yards up the road.

Teddy turned his head as he saw Sandie recognize the Emmerdale vehicle. He was ready with a rude gesture but to his surprise Jack Sugden gave a friendly wave as he drove by. Jack was mindful of what Matt had said, that he ought not to act the heavy stepfather.

'Ooh, I'm in favour, after all,' Teddy crowed as Jack disappeared up the hill. 'You been telling him not to interfere?'

'I spoke to Mum about it. I expect she had a word.'

'That's good.'

'Don't say it like that.'

'I'm not getting at her. I'm glad she spoke up for you. Funny she should have to, that's all. You ready to risk it again?'

'What?' She was swinging her satchel against her leg, looking down, pretending not to understand.

'Come out for the evening. Go to a disco – a proper disco, in Hotten.'

'I might,' she murmured.

'Have to ask permission?'

'No!' she said hotly. 'Don't go on about it, Teddy!'

'All right, all right. I didn't come here to start a row. You coming out tonight, then?'

'How do you come to be here, any road? Shouldn't you be working?'

'Took an hour off,' he told her with nonchalance. 'My own boss, I am. How about it?'

'I'll see how I feel. Might be at lane-end around seven-thirty – you never can tell.'

'Huh!' he said, impressed despite himself by her hard-to-get tactics. 'I might be there too. You never can tell. And now I better get back to them spuds.'

At the end of the day's work Joe was tidying up a few points about the game chicks with Seth. October wasn't so far off after all, and he wanted a good showing when shooting started. Teddy Hooson put his head round the door. 'You wanted me?' he enquired.

'Aye, I did. Come in.' To Seth he said, 'I'll see what I can do about cutting down disturbance, but you've got to understand agriculture has to go on.'

'If I don't get more peace for them pheasants I'm going to write to the bosses in Spalding! It's them as wants to shoot, and it's them as got to give me the right conditions to provide good shooting,' Seth said in wrath.

'That's up to you. You get off home now.'

Seth strode out, his old spectacles flashing with indignation. Teddy came forward, grinning at the scene.

'How's the spraying going?' Joe enquired, his attention apparently on some papers on his desk.

'All right. About half done.'

'No trouble with the machine?'

'No, it works like a dream, easy as pie.'

'And you've kept at it all day?'

'Of course,' Teddy said. 'What else would I be doing?'

Joe looked up and gave him a cool glance. 'That's what I want to know. You were away from the job when I passed by this afternoon. Where were you?'

'Oh – ah – ' said Teddy, as if recollecting. 'I . . . er . . . got an urgent call. You know? You must have come by while I were in the bushes.' He wasn't bothered by the questioning. He knew he could talk his way out of anything.

'How long did this take?' Joe enquired.

'Bit longer than usual,' said Teddy. He allowed himself an apologetic grin. 'I were taken bad.'

'Sorry about that,' said Joe. 'But how long?'

'Not going to dock it off me wages, are you?' Teddy asked, still not sensing any danger.

'Fifteen minutes?' Joe insisted. 'Not twenty, surely.'

'About fifteen . . . yeh.'

Joe leaned back in his chair, arms straight, palms outstretched on the desk. 'I called there three times over the space of an hour and each time the machine was in the same place and you were nowhere about. Where were you?'

'I told you,' said Teddy, going red. 'Matter of fact, I had to go twice. I said I was took bad.'

Joe shook his head. 'Look, Teddy, don't mess me about. You left the job and you left the machine where anyone could have fiddled with it. Now, where were you?'

'I had to drink me tea, didn't I?'

'Even though you were feeling bad? And how long did it take you to drink your tea? Ten minutes? That still leaves thirty-five unaccounted for. Where were you?'

'I've told you.'

'You have not told me,' Joe said. 'You're lying, Teddy.'

Teddy's temper exploded. 'Don't you bloody call me a liar!'

'I'm calling you by the right name. You're not telling me the truth and that makes you a liar.'

'Shut your gob!' shouted Teddy.

Joe stared at him. An extraordinary silence fell. Then Joe said, 'You're fired.'

'Now you look here –'

'You're fired. Get out!'

Teddy hesitated. He measured Joe with his eye. No use trying the soft soap on this one.

'What are you waiting for? Get out.'

'All right,' Teddy said, 'but you haven't heard the end of this!'

As he stormed out, he ran into Jackie Merrick. 'Hey, what's up wi' you?' Jackie cried as they collided and Teddy brushed by.

'That Joe Sugden,' snarled Teddy, 'he thinks he's fired me! But I tell you, he's got another think coming to him!'

'What happened? Hey, Teddy, what happened?'

'None of your business! I'm off down the pub, drown me sorrows.'

'I'll buy you a half, Teddy,' Jackie said, eager to find out what had caused the storm that was plain on the other lad's face.

In the Woolpack Teddy unbent enough to relate his side of the story. 'All I did was nip off for a minute to have a chat wi' Sandie,' he said. He felt sure Jackie would be on his side if it was to do with his sister. 'That's no cause to sack anyone!'

'But you didn't tell him that. You said . . .'

'I know what I said. It's not a sacking matter, whatever I did. They'll back me up at Spalding, any road. No one's ever complained of my work there.'

'That's different. They might not have had any cause, there,' Jackie said incautiously.

'There's no cause now!'

'It's the way bosses look at it. Nipping off to speak to a girl.'

'But he didn't know that! As far as he knows I were took sick. Inhuman, that is, taking it out of a man because he's too sick! Looked at that way, he'd no cause to sack me.'

'So why did he?'

''Cos he's a berk, that's why!'

Jackie smothered a grin. 'What you mean is, he didn't believe you.'

'He was looking for a way to get at me. Bet he's in cahoots with your Dad, getting at me over Sandie.'

'Oh, come on, Teddy,' Jackie said, unable to go along with this fable. 'Joe wouldn't –'

'Don't tell me you're going to take a Sugden's side?' Teddy cried in disgust. 'You've a lot to complain of yourself.'

'That's different –'

'You can bet they stick together! Your stepdad didn't want me seeing Sandie and he got Joe to find a way to get rid of me.'

Jackie shook his head. 'You don't believe that, do you?'

'Don't I? Don't I? Well, I'll tell you summat. Whether I do or not, I can make others believe it!'

He meant to get in first with his tale to Alan Turner, but he was unlucky because Alan was at that moment talking to Joe.

'You sacked him?' he cried in disbelief.

'I had no option. If you'd been there you'd have done the same.'

Alan shook his head and sat down on the leather sofa, already foreseeing all kinds of trouble over this matter. 'Tell me exactly what happened.'

'I was passing the forty acre and saw the tractor and sprayer unattended in the corner,' Joe reported. 'I went to it but couldn't find Teddy anywhere. I went back three times in the next hour and he still wasn't there.' He described the rest of the events as concisely as he could. 'He told me to shut my gob so I fired him.'

Alan reached for his cigarette case, selected a cigarette, and thought about it.

'What else could I do, Alan?'

'There are established rules for dismissing staff. You've broken them all, Joe.' He raised a hand as Joe was about to protest. 'Firstly *we* can't sack him as he belongs to Spalding.'

'We're all N.Y. Estates!'

'Legally he has been sacked by N.Y., insofar as you represent N.Y. But within the firm it is not the done thing. The correct procedure is to refer the matter to the division concerned. In Hooson's case, Spalding. But it only makes matters worse because the way you've done it, you've given him a cast iron case of unfair dismissal. He could take the company to the tribunal and he'd win.'

'Win! I don't see how! I'm not saying I'm God, but I am the manager. He can't be allowed to speak to me like that.'

'There are procedures, Joe,' Turner said in his somewhat

76

prissy way. 'They're laid down in agreement with the union and we are bound to follow them.'

'You mean I should have sat there and let him cheek me?'

'You should have cautioned him. Suspended him, if you like. But you should not have sacked him on the spot.'

'But he'd been skiving off work!'

'You've no proof of that.'

'I have proof! He wasn't there!'

'You should have listened to his explanation.'

'I did. It was a pack of lies!'

'And that's the next point. You shouldn't have called him a liar. That's a very nasty accusation.'

'But it's a fact!'

'I don't know whether the tribunal or union would agree with that, especially as you yourself admit you were a bit . . . well . . . steamed up.'

Joe had used up all his indignation in his protests. He looked at Turner now, and realized he was going to get no support from him.

'So what now?' he asked.

'You'll have to reinstate him, Joe.'

'What? Over my dead body!'

'You'll have to. And Joe – let's hope he accepts your apology.'

Chapter Six

About that time, Dolly and Matt were in their room getting ready for their date with Turner. Dolly was worrying about what to wear.

'D'you think I should be dressy? Drinks . . . Does that mean a cocktail dress?'

'Have you got a cocktail dress?' Matt enquired with a faint grin.

'Well, no.'

'That settles that, then, doesn't it!'

'Matt, be serious. We want to make a good impression.'

'You always make a good impression, love.'

'But this is different, Matt. If he don't like the look of us, he may change his mind.'

'He's seen us about in Beckindale often enough, love. If he don't know by now what we're like, he never will.'

She couldn't take it as philosophically as her husband. She'd had rather a bad day. During the afternoon she'd felt it only fair to tell Annie that she and Matt were to have a chat with Alan Turner about the possibility of renting a cottage, and it had not gone well.

'I wish she hadn't made me feel I'm deserting her,' she mourned now as she rummaged about in the bottom of the wardrobe for the belt, which had slipped off the dress.

'She can't help being upset, Dolly. She don't want us to go.'

'I'd have been glad if the ground had opened and swallowed me when I'd said it.'

Matt, tying his tie before the mirror, turned to her. 'Look, love, do you want to change your mind?'

'No, of course not. I just wish it didn't leave her so . . . sort of swamped.' She paused, having been on the edge of saying 'swamped by strangers'. Say what you like, the Merricks were strangers to Annie; oddly enough once Matt and Dolly left, Annie would be, so to speak, outnumbered in her own home.

This uncomfortable thought made her plunge into speech. 'Do I look like I'd make a respectable tenant?'

'Not only respectable – when he sees you he'll put the rent up!' Matt teased. And indeed, in her soft pink dress and little white scarf, Dolly looked good enough to eat.

'How much do you think he'll ask?' she wondered aloud.

'No idea, lass. I've never rented anything in my life before. This is a new business for me.'

'I've only rented rooms, never a cottage or a home. How'll we know whether it's the right rent or not?'

'By whether we can afford it,' Matt grinned.

'Well, we don't have to leap at it right away, do we? We can play it cool.' She looked at him with doubt. 'He won't offer it to anyone else if we don't seem keen?'

'How'd I know, Dolly? I expect there's a load of folk would want it if we didn't.'

'Oh, Lord!' She gave her hair a nervous brush or two. Then she stopped, staring at her reflection. 'You don't suppose he'd sell it, do you?'

He shook his head emphatically. 'Farmers don't sell their cottages except for really big prices. They can always use accommodation for their own workers if they can't get above the going rate for the place.' He came up behind her, to look at her face in the mirror. 'Don't let's go jumping any guns, lass. We don't know for sure whether he's going to offer it to us to rent.'

'But that's why he's seeing us, isn't it?'

'He didn't exactly say that. He just said, talk it over.'

'Oh, heck!' she cried, turning suddenly and burying her head against his shoulder. 'What'll we do if he won't let us have it?'

He held her close, dropping a little kiss on her head. 'Manage, love, like we always have.'

She nodded without looking up.

'At least,' he pointed out, 'we're not being pushed out here. Ma doesn't want us to go. She'd rather stuff us in a cupboard than lose what she calls her family.'

There was something in his voice that made her face him. She looked into his eyes. 'Would you rather stay, Matt?'

He took a moment before answering. He knew it was important for her to understand how he felt. This was a big step they were thinking of and they needed to be of one mind.

'I've had it going through my head for days now,' he said. 'It's time we had our own roof. At first I couldn't come to grips wi' the notion – this has been my home so long, leaving it seemed like a kind of exile. But then I thought of the baby, and realized that in a way . . . sounds funny, when I say it out loud . . . He'd never really know which of us was his Mum and Dad, there'd be so many all around him. And I thought, He's *ours* – happen it's selfish, but I want our own home for our own baby.'

She nodded agreement, went up on tiptoe to kiss him, and linked arms to set out on this momentous visit.

Turner was waiting for them with eagerness. He had his campaign all planned out. Pat Merrick had tidied up the study and even put some flowers on his desk, so that the

79

place looked more like a home and less like an office. He himself had changed into a lounge suit, in honour of the occasion. He had a feeling that Dolly Skilbeck would appreciate such niceties.

He welcomed them in the moment they stepped out of the Land-Rover. 'Just on time, I've got the scotch warming in the oven!'

Dolly recognized this as a joke and gave a little laugh. Matt, on whom it was lost, followed his wife into the old study which he hadn't seen since it used to belong to George Verney, former 'squire' of Beckindale. It was an impressive room even now it was an office. Despite all his resolutions not to be taken at a disadvantage, Matt began to feel nervous.

'Scotch? Cinzano? Sherry? Name your poison – I've some rather nice Beaujolais, if you'd care for that.'

They settled for the wine. It was, in fact, very good. Dolly knew it was a compliment to be offered something of that calibre, and began to feel a little more confident.

'Now let me put you in the picture a little bit as regards N.Y.,' Turner said, holding his wine up to the light while leaning back to regard it. 'You realize, I'm sure, that N.Y. are into high-profit farming. That's led to some friction hereabouts, and I don't deny our object is to make profits. But then, it's the same with every farmer.' He looked enquiringly at Matt who, knowing he must be polite, nodded agreement. In any case, he actually did agree. Emmerdale couldn't go on unless it made them a decent living.

'But though we want big profits, we're in a position not to need them immediately. In other words, we can have long-term projects which offer big profits but at some future date.'

'That's right,' Matt said. He was going to say, 'That's Jack's idea about Hathersage,' but decided against it. It wasn't tactful to mention Jack to Alan Turner. Not if they wanted to get a cottage off him.

Dolly, who had been listening intently, was beginning to wonder what this had to do with her. She was here to find out about the cottage, not hear a lecture on farming methods. But Turner was their host so she sat looking interested.

'As you know,' he continued, 'N.Y. have not made much use of sheep as a profit source. Joe is interested in them, but so far we've not utilized his experience on that score.' Matt smothered a grin. 'We' – that meant, us, N.Y. Estates. Turner fancied himself as part of the hierarchy of N.Y., it seemed.

'But Joe recently did a remarkable study for us. He took the land over the Struggle as a specimen. He showed how it was under-used, worked out profitable ratings, and came up with the answer that we could graze another hundred sheep there.'

'Aye,' mused Matt, 'there's short grass there in plenty among them boulders. Have to watch out for damage to the hooves in wet weather – gets slippy up there, sheep could knock themselves.'

'Maybe, maybe,' Turner agreed. He got up. 'Let me top you up.'

'Nay, nay, I'm fine.'

'Dolly?'

'We-ell . . .'

'Do have more, I'm going to.' He filled her glass, refilled his own. He sat down, but more alert, not leaning back this time. 'The plan is to have a really big herd. We'd take up Joe's idea of another hundred, but I think that's a conservative estimate when you think of other areas of short grass we have within the estate.'

'Well, you've got a good old shepherd in Jesse,' Matt said. 'There's not many round these parts could teach him owt about sheep.' Privately he was thinking, Jesse won't thank 'em for making him stomp among those rocks – he's getting a bit past it.

'I hear you're pretty good,' Turner said.

Matt smiled. 'We've all got our special ways.'

'I expect you think he's the best shepherd in the district, Mrs Skilbeck.'

'I always hear him well spoken of,' Dolly said, with pride. 'And that's why he's got a right to a decent house. You didn't say for sure, Mr Turner – has Tolly's got three bedrooms?'

Turner nodded. 'Nice sizeable ones too. In fact, it's an excellent place all round, and though the Tollys had let it go a bit, we've done necessary repairs. You know the house, of course?'

'Only from the outside,' Dolly said.

'I've been in, but while the Tollys were there – and it were years ago,' added Matt.

'Then I must arrange for you to look it over,' Turner murmured, holding out enticement. 'You might find the kitchen a bit basic but I'm sure there'd be no difficulty in getting the company to modernize it into something more like a housewife's dream.'

Dolly caught Matt's eye. He raised his eyebrows in slight bewilderment. 'Does that mean you're willing to let us have it?' she asked, keeping her voice from trembling only with a great effort.

Turner hesitated a moment before responding. No reason to let them think it would be easy. 'I have no personal objection as to renting, though of course the final decision must be with the company. I will put it to them, however.'

'And . . . er . . . the rent, Mr Turner? Have you any idea of what it'd be?' Turner seemed to be thinking about that. 'Just a rough idea,' Matt urged.

'I don't suppose it would be cheap.' He hesitated, as if about to raise a delicate point. 'You have a family coming, I understand. That makes it rather urgent.'

'Not that urgent,' Dolly said, wondering if she should say there were still six months to go. 'But we do want somewhere for when the baby comes, don't we, Matt?'

'We're able to pay a reasonable rent, Mr Turner. And if the modernizing is likely to put it high, we could do that ourselves.'

'Yes, yes . . . I've heard you have considerable skill as a builder and decorator.' He broke off, drank some wine, and seemed to be mulling something over. 'It's just occurred to me, Matt . . . Jesse retires in about ten months or so. If you were willing to take his place you could have the house rent free – completely modernized.' Matt made a muffled sound. 'We pay very high wages for good men,' he added.

Matt and Dolly were staring at each other in bewilderment.

To let the notion sink in, Turner rose and fetched the wine bottle. He poured wine into Matt's almost empty glass. 'You don't have to give your answer now. Think it over. There is a lot in its favour, you know. You'd have a free house, a first class wage, absolute security *and* you'd be more or less your own boss, running your herd with money available to buy the very finest sheep so as to build the best flock in the country!'

After that, it was clear to see, conversation was at an end. Turner felt something like sympathy for Matt Skilbeck, who seemed so stunned he could hardly take in what was going on around him. His wife recovered more quickly, so that she was able to make polite conversation until they could decently take their leave.

'Thanks for the wine, Mr Turner. It was really nice.'

'Oh, call me Alan, please. If we're going to be associates, Matt and I, we'll be on first name terms.'

'I dunno that I –'

'Sleep on it, Matt. It's a good offer. It's – well, it's like putting your future on a new footing, isn't it? And with a family coming, you have to think of the future, don't you? Well, bye-bye for the present. Let me know what you think, will you. I don't want to hurry you, but if the company follow up this idea of Joe's, it may be that they'll want to make a decision about the future of Tolly's Farmhouse.'

'Yes, we understand that, Mr Turner – Alan – we'll give it a lot of thought. Goodnight.'

They walked down the drive in a daze. After they'd walked a while Matt said suddenly, 'It was a scheme! He had it all worked out that way afore he ever invited us!'

'What – you mean about the cottage?'

'Aye, he never intended to offer it for rent. The devious –'

'Nay, Matt, even if you're right, he clearly wanted to make the offer of the job.'

'Why couldn't he just say so, instead of scrambling all round Carr's Crag to come out wi' it?'

'You'd have said no right off if he'd started that way.'

'Well, that would have been better than getting us all hopeful!'

She let a long moment go by before she spoke. 'You wouldn't think of leaving Emmerdale then, Matt?'

He turned his head suddenly. In the dusk it was impossible to read his face. And neither could he read in hers what the question meant.

'We would be leaving Emmerdale if we got somewhere else to live . . .' he said.

'That's not what I mean. I meant, work somewhere else.'

Very slowly he said, 'I've never . . . never even thought on it . . . Not afore tonight.'

And there she left it, knowing there was too much at stake to hurry over.

Joe was in the Woolpack, chatting to Henry Wilks. Henry had been witness to the conversation earlier in the evening between Jackie Merrick and Teddy Hooson but only heard part of it. When he queried with Joe if there'd been trouble, Joe had no hesitation in telling him. He wanted Henry's opinion on the rightness of his view.

'Well, Turner's right over one thing,' Henry said with a sigh. 'You can't fire a man on the spot like that. These new regulations make that out of the question.'

'You mean you've got to tolerate a liar and an insubordinate employee?'

'Nay, lad, from what you tell me the facts are against Hooson. Spalding would have to take some action – dock his wages, or summat, just to hold the line against skiving employees. And I can't say as Alan comes well out of it. The least he could have done was send the boy back to Spalding – he might have preferred to tell him to forget the whole incident but at least he ought not to leave you holding the bag.'

'You mean Hooson should get his job back?'

'What you don't understand is, he's not lost his job. You can't fire him, not without notice and due discussion. The law's against you. But Alan's wrong to tell you you've got to eat humble pie and personally reinstate him. He ought to see your side of it.'

Joe looked moodily into his beer mug. 'There's summat

84

funny about Alan, you know. I can't quite put my finger on it. If it came to the crunch, I wouldn't trust him very far . . .'

He looked at Henry, who made no move to defend the man against this strong criticism. Joe went on in an uncertain tone: 'I get the impression he's always out for Number One.'

'His predecessor warned you, didn't he? Life in the agrobusiness is rough and tough.'

'I wouldn't mind if Alan was a bit rough. My complaint is, he's too smooth by far!' Joe frowned. 'And I tell you summat, Henry. If he wants Teddy Hooson reinstated, he'll have to do it himself. I won't, and if Alan don't like it, he can sack me!'

He still held to this view next morning when Alan broached the subject anew. 'You have to see that for the benefit of good employer-employee relationships –'

'As far as I'm concerned there's no relationship between Hooson and me,' Joe said with complete firmness. 'I sacked him and he's no longer an employee.'

'Don't be absurd, Joe! He's got to be reinstated.'

Joe shook his head.

'I have a job to do and I'm doing it. I'm trying to repair the damage. You must understand!' Turner begged.

'I understand that you'd rather believe Hooson than me.'

'Nothing of the kind!'

'Then why do you keep saying his version has to be taken into account? I told you what happened!'

'You have to take into account that you might have made a mistake about the times –'

'I made no mistake. That lad is lying in his teeth. He was away from the job for over an hour.'

'All right, all right,' Turner agreed, throwing up his hands, 'but you can't sack a man for that.'

'I didn't sack him for that.'

'Well, when he explained –'

'He didn't explain, he lied. And when I told him he was lying, he was downright rude.'

'You sacked him,' Turner said with heavy patience,

'because he cheeked you.'

'Too right I did! If I cheeked you, would you like it?'

'I hope I wouldn't lose my temper, Joe. I certainly wouldn't sack you on the spot.'

Joe drew in a deep breath, got up, and walked to the window where he stared out at the garden of Home Farm. Alan, taking this as a sign of second thoughts, went on in his most winning tone. 'It's no good shutting your eyes to it, Joe, you acted hastily and put me in a very awkward position. Leaving aside the awkward point of Hooson's being on Spalding's roster, there is no doubt that if Hooson takes this to an industrial tribunal he would win . . . to say nothing of trouble he could cause through his union. We have no option but to reinstate him.'

'That's your decision, Alan,' Joe said over his shoulder. 'You're the boss.'

'Good . . . good . . . I knew you'd see it sensibly. You'll tell him then?'

Joe swung about. 'No, I won't,' he said. 'You want him reinstated, Alan, you do it. And if that makes it awkward for you, I'll resign. Or you can sack me – I don't mind. I won't take you to a tribunal if you do, it's not my way. But I'm not going to eat humble pie to a little berk who I know is a liar and who spoke to me in a way that deserved a sock on the jaw.'

Alan hesitated. He was faced with a direct choice – support Joe and the firing of Teddy Hooson, or cover his own retreat and smooth things over. It was a test, if he had but known it, and in Joe's eyes he failed.

'Don't be silly, Joe,' he faltered, foreseeing the uproar at Spalding if he lost this expert assistant manager.

Joe shrugged. 'I mean it,' he said.

'I meant . . . don't be silly, it's not that important. *I'll* tell Hooson he's reinstated if you'd rather not. We don't want to make an issue of it and you're too good a man to lose over a boy who'll be off our hands in a week or two anyway.'

'I'll get out and about then,' Joe said, making for the door without thanking Turner for his intentions.

'And I'll tell Hooson to get on with the spraying of the potatoes – is that it?'

'It's what he's here for,' Joe replied with no sign of unbending. Then, to Turner's encouragement, he paused. Some sign of relenting, perhaps? But no. Joe said, still cool: 'Have you seen Matt yet?'

'Yes, it was last night, you know,' Turner said, brightening at the recollection.

'And you offered him the job? What did he say?'

'He seemed very interested. And his wife was very taken at the idea of Tolly's Farmhouse. When they've had time to think it over, I'll take them there and show them the house. I may give Matt a ring this afternoon.'

'I see,' said Joe, and went out.

Outside, Teddy Hooson was leaning against the wall of the terrace waiting to be summoned. Although he looked indolent, he couldn't help eyeing Joe with some anxiety. He knew his job was safe, but all the same, it'd be a bit of a black mark on his record if he was shipped back to Spalding a couple of days after he was lent out, and with a note to say he'd been playing hooky.

Joe ignored him, went to his Land-Rover. Teddy, not lacking in courage whatever else might have been in question, went up to him.

'You'd best go in the office. Mr Turner wants to see you.' Spotting Jack drive into the courtyard, he walked away. Teddy stood watching him. No sign that Mr Turner had had him on the carpet. Could it be Joe was going to win this bout?

Jack Sugden was getting out of the Emmerdale Land-Rover. His wife, Jackie Merrick's mother, got out the other side. She worked in Turner's office, Teddy had learned. The men exchanged greetings. Joe said, 'You know, if it's inconvenient to drop Pat off every morning, you could give me a ring. I could fetch her.'

'Might do some morning if we're extra busy. But today I wanted to return the loan of the di-methoate. Ours has just been delivered.'

'Okay, sling 'em in the back. I'll drop 'em in the store as I go by.' Joe got aboard and drove off.

Teddy, having watched his enemy off the premises, went in to hear his fate. He was soon reassured. Alan Turner didn't want trouble, even if his pal Joe Sugden was ready to square up to him. Within half an hour Teddy was up on the big fields of N.Y.'s potato crop, turning the tractor for its first run along the rows.

Jackie Merrick, on the way to fetch supplies of wire netting, saw him from the other side of the field and was waved to come over for a word. 'Thought you'd be off to Siberia by now,' he joked as he came up to the side of the tractor.

Teddy leaned out of the high window. 'Nah!' he said in scorn. 'That Alan Turner knows which side his bread's buttered! He didn't want trouble. They can't just fire you, you know!'

To his surprise Jackie frowned. 'That don't make it right, though, does it – just skiving off work?'

'Ho! What's an hour or two to them? Loaded, ain't they, N.Y. Estates? Any road, whose side are you on? You don't love the Sugdens, do you?'

'They're all right.'

'What!'

'Except for Jack. I got nothing to say for him.'

'I should hope not,' Teddy said, remembering the humiliation of Jack's treatment. 'Say, how's Sandie?'

'All right.'

'We went to a disco last night.'

'So I heard.'

'She's great. I go for her.'

Jackie looked perplexed, then came out with, 'Look, don't keep her out so late. Ma don't like it.'

'Ho, ho, too bad! You do everything your Ma tells you?'

'Oh, dry up.'

'Your Ma gets her orders from Jack Sugden, you can be sure! Bossy-boots, that's him. And I'm going to get even with him for sticking his nose in where it's not wanted, don't you worry – and bossy Joe Sugden too!'

'You'll have your hands full,' Jackie said, grinning at the absurdity of it. 'Fighting two sides at once, you'll be.'

'How d'you mean?'

'Well, Joe's *for* N.Y. Estates, Jack's against.'

Teddy shrugged and made a dismissive gesture, as if to say he was so clever he could handle them with his hands tied behind his back. 'Here,' he said, 'you got a key to that caravan still?'

'As a matter of fact, I have. What of it?'

'Not bad, eh. Could be nice and cosy there, you and Jane, me and Sandie. Quite a treat!'

'Look, I got to get on,' Jackie said, suddenly anxious to escape. 'Seth'll be wondering where I got to.'

After the dinner break Alan Turner came out to ensure that all was going well with the spraying. Teddy was refilling the sprayer at the storehouse. Alan wandered about making an inspection, and at once espied di-methoate in a different container. He tapped the two big bottles. 'Where did these come from? They're not ours.'

'It's some Emmerdale returned, Mr Turner, I saw Mr Sugden give it to Joe this morning.'

'Returned? I didn't know we'd been lending chemicals to Emmerdale.'

Teddy shrugged, as if meaning nowt to do with me. Alan drove off, to tackle Joe about it. 'Since when do we lend materials to Emmerdale, Joe?' he demanded.

'Materials? Meaning what?'

'There's two demi-johns of di-meth in the store that come from them, I hear.'

'Oh, that. Well, why not? It's just being good neighbours, and you're always saying we have to build up good public relations.'

'There are people who would respond better to good neighbourliness than your brother Jack,' Alan said, but let it go. Joe was right. Farmers lent things to one another; if they did not, the farming community would grind to a halt.

But the incident had given Teddy Hooson the perfect idea for getting his own back on his enemies. That evening, when all the rest of the farm labour force had gone home, Teddy drove in his violently painted little car to the isolated spot where the chemicals store stood. He had the key in his possession; he had been trusted to work on his own with the spraying.

Inside, he took an empty di-meth keg of the kind Alan Turner had obtained for N.Y. Estates. Into it he emptied the contents of the plastic container from Emmerdale, also di-methoate. He did the same again, so that he had two empty containers from Emmerdale which had formerly held di-meth.

From the corner where Joe had stacked them, he took the bottles of Paraquat.

Very carefully, he emptied the Paraquat into the Emmerdale containers and put on the screw tops. Then, as a perfect finishing touch, he damaged the hasp of the lock with his clasp-knife before re-locking the door and driving away.

Chapter Seven

When Matt and Dolly reached home the evening of their talk with Turner, they found the kitchen in the state of crowdedness that had become usual. Jack was doing accounts on the kitchen table, Pat was tacking together a blouse for Sandie. Sandie was upstairs doing homework but her brother was rooting about in the larder after the ingredients for a sandwich: he seemed to be always hungry. Sam was reading and drowsing in his armchair. Annie was knitting across the hearth from him.

Dolly knew that Annie was burning to know the result of their conversation with Alan Turner, but of course would never ask, certainly not in front of all the family. For her part, Dolly didn't want to talk about it. She felt weary and unsettled. She said to Matt, 'Cup of cocoa?'

'Nay, I've had enough for tonight,' he said, feeling full of wine.

'Then I'm for bed.' She wasn't sleepy; she just didn't feel like general conversation in the kitchen.

'Righto, love.' After goodnights all round they went upstairs. Matt took off the jacket of his good suit and began to loosen his tie. He'd be glad to get out of such gear. He never felt entirely at ease in a suit.

'What a *crush* it seems down there,' Dolly said as she put his jacket on a hanger.

'Aye, right enough. Funny that. It's a big enough room for all of us. It just seems somehow . . .'

'We've always been able to spread ourselves. Now we

can't spread without disturbing Pat's dressmaking or Sandie's exercise books.'

He came to her and put his hands on her shoulders. 'Hold on, lass. It's not as serious a problem as that.'

'There isn't really a problem, Matt,' she said, looking directly into his eyes. 'All that's lacking is the will to face up to the answer.'

He nodded. 'That's what problems always are, isn't it? I mean, there's always an answer of sorts. It's finding the one you want as causes the trouble!'

She moved away from under his touch. 'You don't want to leave Emmerdale,' she said, and it was almost an accusation.

'I'd rather not – ' And as Dolly was about to make a retort he went on quickly: 'But that don't mean I wouldn't leave, if it were t'best answer.'

She sighed. It was impossible to have an argument with Matt. 'I can't see that there is any other answer. If we're ever going to have a home of our own, that is.'

'And I promise you, love,' he replied in his calm, gentle tone, 'if it's the only way, I'll do it.'

Next afternoon young Jackie Merrick asked Seth for permission to go to the caravan to see if there were any letters. His mother hadn't yet got round to filling in a form at the Post Office to say they'd moved. He found one from the man he considered as his real father, Tom Merrick, painting a wonderful picture of high life in Aberdeen after a stint on the oil rig.

He was sitting on the steps reading this when Teddy Hooson appeared. 'Love letter?' he enquired, leaning alongside Jackie against the van.

'It's from me Dad . . . I mean, Tom . . . What you doing here?'

'Spying out the land.'

'What for?'

'See if I can improve it before our party.'

'Oh, well, as to that, Teddy – '

'Don't say you're backing out?'

'I never backed in,' Jackie said with a grin. 'It was all your idea.'

'Well, it's still a great idea. Ten o'clock at night, stars

showing in the sky, transistor giving out with the old smoochy-koochy, and a six-pack of lager – lovely!'

'Shouldn't you be working?' Jackie enquired, to avoid replying to the suggestion.

'I'm off in the bushes 'cos I've got stomach-ache. Ha-ha, joke.' But Teddy did actually laugh. 'Told you I'd do Sugden, didn't I? He didn't half get a wigging from old Turner and now he's going round looking as if he's swallowed a dose of Paraquat! He had to accept my reinstatement – but he's got worse coming to him.' Teddy laughed again and slapped Jackie on the shoulder. 'You wait, mate! You'll see! I've landed both the Sugdens in it, put them right in it!'

Jackie got up, to avoid being matily slapped by a lad he was beginning to dislike quite keenly. 'Why? What you up to?'

'That'd be telling, wouldn't it! But you'll enjoy the outcome.' He paused, eyeing Jackie, who didn't seem all that enthusiastic. 'You wouldn't mind seeing 'em in the slurry, would you?'

'I told you,' Jackie said in an easy tone, 'I don't have anything against 'em – only Jack, and that's –'

'Huh!' sneered Teddy. 'Falling for the cosy home-life bit? Buttering you up, are they? Slippers by the fire, cocoa at bed-time?'

Jackie was irritated. 'I don't see how you've got so much against 'em. You asked for what you got from Joe, and as to Jack –'

'I don't take that treatment lying down!' Teddy cut in. 'Anyone gets the knife in me, he gets it back with interest, and you can bet on that.'

'All you'll do is land yourself in worse trouble.'

'Me? Me? There's no way they can hurt me. Got a tribunal to threaten 'em with, ain't I? And me union. Any road,' and he kicked carelessly at a pebble by his foot, 'I'm thinking of jacking all this in. Fed up of being stuck in little pokey places. Fancy seeing life a bit, getting around. Hey, Jackie, ever thought of joining the army?'

Jackie moved off. 'I like what I'm doing,' he said. 'And I got to get back – Seth only let me off for ten minutes.'

'Well, hang on – what about Sandie? What about this

party?'

'Anything you want to fix with Sandie is your affair.'

A sound overlaid his words. Joe's Land-Rover drove up. Joe got out and surveyed them. To Teddy he said, 'Well? What's the excuse this time?'

'I was attending to the needs of nature,' Teddy said, with a sidelong wink at Jackie.

'You must have the loosest bowels in the history of man. Get back to your tractor.'

'Yes, sir,' Teddy said, and this time his wink to Jackie was open and deliberate as he left.

Joe sighed then looked at Jackie. 'And how about you, Jackie?'

'Seth gave me a few minutes to check the letterbox.'

'I see. And what now?'

'I'm to meet him at Home Farm.'

'Right, you can come with me in the Rover. I'm off there myself.'

At the farm he let Jackie alight at Seth's hidey-hole by the stables, then drove up to the door. He found Alan fussing about among the files. 'I wish we could have Pat here every day all day,' he complained. 'It's always easier to lay your hands on what you want when she's here.'

'That's true. And she makes good coffee too,' Joe said with a grin.

'By the way, Joe, do you know anything about a broken hasp on the chemical store-shed?'

'On the – ? Nay, first I've heard of it.'

'Teddy reported it to me this morning. You'd better come with me to take a look. Probably some tramp or something, but it doesn't do to take chances with all that stuff in there.'

When they examined the door, all they could tell was that someone had forced off the bar that went across to pass over the staple, thus by-passing the locked padlock. The door opened easily to the touch. They went into the shed, looked about.

'No signs of anybody kipping here,' Joe remarked.

'Would there be any signs, if he just bedded down on those old sacks?'

'Happen not. Well, I'll get Peters to see to it. Best get

a proper lock put on – otherwise he may come back and do in the new padlock.'

'I leave that with you, then, Joe.'

As they turned to go, Joe said: 'Had a decision from Matt yet?'

'No, I'm not hurrying. Easy does it in this case. I'm going to give him a ring.'

Joe sighed and shrugged.

'And remember, Joe – not a word to anyone.'

'You've already given me my orders on that point,' Joe said with some irritation.

'All right, all right, I'm not doubting your discretion,' Turner responded, backing down as usual at any sign of confrontation. 'I just don't want anything to go wrong with this idea. Head Office will be pleased if I bring it off.'

Annie Sugden, having heard not a word from Matt or Dolly about their evening with Alan Turner, called in at the Woolpack a little before morning opening time, her excuse being that she had a new brand of biscuits to give to Amos as a present. She wanted to give them as a thank you for Amos's help over the wine for the wedding reception.

'Well, that's very kind of you, Annie, very kind indeed,' he said, beaming with pleasure as he surveyed the foiled package. 'From Denmark! Famous, they are, for their cooking. Think of Danish pastries.'

'Put them in an airtight tin, Amos,' Annie warned. 'They lose their crispness in a minute.'

'Right, right, I'll put them in the tin I got from my Auntie Mavis at Christmas.'

He bustled off. Annie sat down in the empty saloon bar and looked at Henry.

'Well?' he said. 'What's the real reason you're here?'

'Nothing escapes you, Henry, does it! I'm right worried. Did you know Dolly and Matt were seeing Alan Turner last night, about a cottage?'

'Nay, heard nowt of that.'

'They went out about seven-thirty, came back about half-nine, Dolly really sort of edgy and Matt with nowt to say. They went straight up to their room. And Henry . . .

they've never mentioned the evening.'

'We-ell,' he replied, 'a bit difficult, having a conversation about anything personal, at your breakfast table these days.'

It was only too true. 'You know Mr Turner's got Tolly Farmhouse empty?'

'Of course. Nice little place. Handy for Emmerdale too, if it comes to that.'

'But they've not said a word, Henry! Don't you think that's funny? I mean – far from trying to have a word in private, Dolly's been practically avoiding me.'

Henry considered the problem. 'Have you asked her about it?'

'No,' she said, shaking her head, 'I've been hard put to it not to, but I didn't want them to think I was busybodying.'

'Well, if they'd got it, they'd have said, wouldn't they? I mean, they'd have been full of it.'

'They're not. They're not pleased and relieved. If anything, they're more anxious-looking than before.'

'Then happen they're too disappointed to talk about it, Annie.'

'Aye, it could be that. But you remember you said there seemed more to it than met the eye, the way Joe was acting?'

'I remember.'

'I've been thinking. Old Jesse is retiring in the spring of next year. They'll want a replacement.'

'Replacement?'

'Aye, lad. And they've already taken Joe away from us. Why shouldn't they try and take Matt?'

The more Henry thought about it after she'd gone, the more it made sense. He glanced at Amos. 'All right if I just pop out for a minute or two, Amos?'

'Mr Wilks! We're just about to open for business!'

'There'll be nobody but Old Walter for the first half hour, Amos, you know that. I'll be back afore it gets busy.'

'I've heard that before, Mr Wilks, if you don't mind me saying so.' Amos was lofty. 'Gone for hours, you are, sometimes.'

'This won't be one of those times. It's important.'

'To who?' Now Amos was eager. He scented a drama.

'To Annie and others we're fond of. I promise, Amos, I won't hang about.'

While his partner was still digesting the information that the problem had to do with Emmerdale, Henry was off out. He got into his car and drove briskly to N.Y. Estates. He had heard Joe saying he'd be at the office.

Joe was there, attending to the paperwork which seemed inevitable these days. Henry said, 'Thinking of coming down to t'Woolpack for a late ploughman's? I were just passing and thought I'd give you a lift.'

Joe gave him a surprised glance. Henry nodded insistently. 'Righto,' Joe said, 'might as well take a break now. See you later, Alan.'

Alan Turner nodded without looking up. He was concocting on paper the terms he'd offer Matt Skilbeck when he rang him later in the day.

'Well, now, what's this all about?' Joe said as they rolled down the drive towards Verney Lane.

'You tell me, lad. What's going on?'

'What's going on where?'

'At Home Farm – about Matt and Dolly.'

'Why?' Joe said too quickly. 'Has owt been settled?'

'I don't even know what there *is* to settle, Joe. Your mother's right worried. They were over Home Farm last night and so far, not a word about it to Annie.' He looked speculatively at Joe and waited for a response, but Joe said nothing. Henry went back to his driving. 'Do you know if N.Y. have offered Matt a job? Annie thinks they may have.'

Joe still said nothing.

'Am I to take it that silence means consent?'

'Why don't Ma ask Matt straight out?' Joe countered.

Henry guided the car into the entrance of a field where hay-making was over and no one was about. He switched the engine off. There was a moment of silence.

'There is summat in it then?'

Joe took his time before he responded. 'If I were working for you, Henry, and you had in mind trying to get the best man for a new department you were starting, would you expect me to support you?'

'Aye, lad,' Henry said immediately.

'Irrespective of whether getting the man might affect other interests you had?'

Henry was nodding. 'All right, Joe. You don't have to say any more, I get the picture.'

Joe smiled with some bitterness. 'I'll remind you that I have told you and Ma more than once over the last few days that I thought Matt and Dolly ought to have that barn, not Jack. But of course, it was probably put down to me wanting to queer Jack's pitch in some way.'

'Nay, now, lad –'

'Oh, I know it's common knowledge that Jack and I don't see eye to eye. But I wouldn't try to do him out of a house just for the fun of it. But as it turns out, it's Matt who's been done out of it. And that's the cause of the trouble.'

'Thank you. I understand now.'

'I hope you do, Henry. And I hope you can do summat about it, because I've had no success!'

'I'll try, Joe. I can only try.' Sighing, Henry put the car in motion once more and drove them both to the Woolpack.

Amos was surprised to see Henry back so soon, and a little disappointed at not being able to read him a lecture on absenteeism. But there was something about the two men that warned him not to be too talkative. He served Joe with a half and a ploughman's lunch. Henry busied himself with other customers. It was noticeable that Henry didn't seem to have anything more to talk over with Joe: on the contrary, he seemed totally taken up with his own thoughts.

As Joe was downing the last of his half and thinking about another, the Woolpack's phone rang. Amos answered. He turned to call: 'Joe! It's Mr Turner for you.'

Although he kept his ear cocked, he could make nothing of Joe's end of the short conversation. Henry, who had been standing by to draw another half for Joe, caught Joe's eye. Joe shook his head and hurried out. Then, bethinking himself that Henry might imagine it was something to do with Matt, he called over his shoulder, 'I'm wanted. Alan's in a tizz. Reckons summat's gone wrong with the potato crop!'

The hot sun of late June had helped the work of the Paraquat spray which Teddy Hooson had put into the tank from the bottles labelled di-methoate. The haulms were showing signs of distress. They were wilting and some leaves were whitened almost like bleaching.

'Well?' Alan Turner said impatiently to Joe as he stooped over the plants.

'There's summat got at 'em – no doubt about that.'

'A pest? Disease? What?'

'I dunno,' Joe confessed. He thought a moment. 'Can't be anything much, can it? They were only sprayed a couple of days ago.'

But Turner was not to be consoled. 'It seems so general! Not just one corner, it's all over the field.'

'It don't make sense. They've been really well looked after.'

'I don't want a history of the tender loving care they've had!' Turner interrupted. 'I want to know what's wrong with 'em now! And how serious it is, and what's to be done.'

'We'll have to have the Ministry men down to take a look.' He moved about, spreading wilted leaves with thumb and forefinger to examine more closely. 'If the idea wasn't so daft . . . I'd say these had been sprayed with weedkiller.'

'Weedkiller?' Turner was aghast. 'What kind of weedkiller?'

'I dunno. Could be any . . . It just looks . . .' Joe stood back, puzzled. 'Only thing to do is have a word wi' the experts.'

'Then have it as quick as you can! There are thousands of pounds involved!'

'They can't all be like this, Alan.'

'There's no time for talking, Joe. Drop everything and get these looked at. Find out what is wrong.'

Joe thought for a moment then pulled up a couple of haulms. 'I'll drive to the lab at Connelton,' he said. 'They'll know in a jiffy what's got at them.'

'I'll be at Home Farm,' Turner said. 'Come straight back

98

there.'

Joe nodded then, as he was moving off, thought of something else. 'Does Head Office know?'

'Of course not! I've only just seen them myself. I came out to take a look round before lunch, see everyone had enough to do before I got going on the afternoon appointments, and what do I find? This!' He flung out a dramatic arm.

'Well, it's a funny business, no doubt about it.'

'Funny? Joe, we'll be laughing the other side of our faces if I have to tell Head Office a thing like this!'

Henry Wilks, collecting empties from the table outside the Woolpack, saw Joe drive past on his way to Connelton. He had just enough time to see that Joe looked worried before he had gone by. Worried . . . So was Henry. Now that the lunchtime session was almost over, he stole a moment to go to the phone.

'Annie? You serving a meal?'

'Nay, they've eaten and gone out again. I'm siding the dishes. What's up, Henry?'

'Is Matt or Dolly with you?'

'No, Matt's up looking at the barley with Jack. They think of harvesting in about two weeks. Dolly's helping Grandad with his flower garden. In fact, there's nobody in the room at the moment but me, as Pat's upstairs tidying.'

'Well, I've had a word with Joe, and what I've learned through a sort of system of nods and winks is that Alan Turner has offered Matt a job, with Tolly's Farmhouse as tied cottage.'

'Oh dear . . . Henry . . .'

'I know, Annie, it's a bait Matt can hardly refuse. He's got Dolly and the bairn to think on.'

'Aye. You're right. We never gave enough thought to that, did we?'

'We can't afford to lose Matt, Annie.'

'No, we can't.'

'This is just to let you know the situation. I'll come up later to see what we can do.'

To his consternation, when Henry put the phone down and turned, it was to find Amos almost at his elbow. For once, Amos looked apologetic. 'I wasn't meaning to listen, Mr Wilks. I couldn't help it, being on the rounds for ashtrays.'

It wasn't a time for kid gloves. 'Don't go gossiping on what you've heard, then.'

At once Amos was offended. 'That is no way to speak to a partner, Mr Wilks. As a publican and journalist I know what's confidential and what isn't, without having my character slurred at.'

'No slur intended, Amos. I was just laying it on the line. I don't want this talked about. Understand?'

'I do. And you're right, Mr Wilks. I never trusted that N.Y. lot, never. But all the same, you can trust Matt Skilbeck. He's not a man as would leave anyone in the lurch, let alone Annie.'

'It's not as simple as that, Amos,' Henry said, remembering the special fondness his partner had for Matt and Dolly. 'Matt's got a family to think of now.'

Matt was at that moment thinking of his family. He expected to hear from Alan Turner any minute now, and he needed to know what he was going to say. He and Jack had walked round the ten acres of barley and decided that if the weather continued as hot and fine as at present, the harvest could begin in two weeks.

'All right if I go off for an hour or two now?' he asked Jack.

'Of course it's all right. You don't have to ask me.'

'I don't want you to think I was leaving you with the work while I took free time.'

'I know you better than that, Matt.' Jack was about to walk on, to look at the sheep up on the slopes, but had a thought. 'Did you have any luck over Tolly's Farmhouse?' he enquired.

'That's what I'm going about.'

'Oh, in that case . . . good luck!' Jack strolled on, oblivious. Matt watched him in exasperation. How could he *not* know that Matt was under the strain of a momentous decision about Tolly's Farmhouse?

At Sam's flower garden Matt found Dolly working at the weeds. He touched her on the shoulder and motioned with his head for her to come a little way off, out of the hearing of Sam who was in his little greenhouse.

'Dolly, I'm expecting Mr Turner to ring any minute –'

'Is that why you've come down from t'fields?'

'Nay, lass. I can't come to grips with it in time to tell him what we've decided.'

'Matt –'

'I feel I need to talk it over with someone.'

'You could talk it over with me, love.'

'I don't mean that, Dolly. I want to talk to someone who can take the long view.'

'Meaning who?'

'I've taken some time off. I'm going to tell Henry about it.'

'You telling him you're taking the job?'

'I'm going to ask his advice.' He could see Dolly stiffen, and went on quickly, 'We owe it to Emmerdale to be honest about this.'

'He'll try to persuade you not to go.'

'Mebbe. He'll understand how the two of us are looking at it.'

'Do you think he will?' she parried, not without bitterness. Henry had money enough to solve most difficulties that might arise in his life.

'I feel I've got to talk to someone and Henry's best. He'll see our point about the barn.'

'And the job?'

'If he can offer an alternative solution, I'll take it.'

'Oh, Matt,' she sighed. But she knew he was right. This was too big a step to take without discussion with someone who could perhaps see more than the two of them could see. What was it called? – like that fellow on telly – lateral thinking. Dolly had done all kinds of thinking over their problem and hated the solution she kept coming up with.

Time and again she had weighed the factors in her mind. If they stayed at Emmerdale, how could they ever find a home of their own? If they left Emmerdale for a home of their own, would Matt ever be happy?

It was a problem to which there seemed to be no pleasing solution.

*

Dolly wasn't the only one with doubts about her own actions. Jackie Merrick was asking advice from Seth on a point that was troubling him.

'D'you reckon Mr Turner should have supported Joe over sacking Teddy Hooson?' he began, the conversation having turned towards Joe's present moody appearance.

'How should I know?'

'But if you were supposed to be in charge and I skived off—'

'What d'you mean, supposed?' Seth said with enough indignation to bristle his droopy moustache. 'I'm the gamekeeper!'

'I mean, put yourself in Joe's position,' Jackie amended hastily. 'Teddy skived off work and when Joe told him off he cheeked him—'

'Nay, nay, fair's fair, lad,' Seth interrupted. 'It's said Joe called the lad a liar and as far as I know that's not been denied.'

'But Teddy *is* a liar,' Jackie said.

'You what?'

'He told Joe he had a stomach upset but it were nowt o't'sort. He was off chatting up our Sandie.'

Seth was amazed. 'How do you know?'

'He told me. And Sandie did too, though of course she didn't know she were tattling on him. He left the tractor stood in the forty acre and met her off the school bus. Well, that's asking for it, isn't it?'

Seth mused over that for a moment. Then he reached behind him for his flask and poured himself a mid-afternoon cup of tea. They were in his hidey-hole not far from the Home Farm stables, with a great deal of working still to do until light failed that evening.

'Well . . . It's over now,' he said, after a satisfactory swallow. 'Be ancient history soon 'cos the lad's off back to Spalding next week.'

Jackie had a can of lemonade for his 'dockey'. He opened it under Seth's disapproving eye. 'Dunno about ancient history,' he said. 'Something new's come up.'

'New?' Seth was alert like a gun dog. 'What's to do, then?'

'Can't be sure. But when I went past the office coming

here, there was a right old barney going on. Couldn't help hearing – they've the windows wide open this warm weather.'

'Go on! Atween Joe and Turner? What about?'

Jackie blushed. 'I didn't stop to earwig, Seth! What d'you take me for?'

Seth leapt up. 'I'd best go and see Mr Turner about those boxes for the game-chicks.'

'But, Seth –'

'You finish your drink and get off up the enclosure. See you there in fifteen minutes.' With that Seth hurried off. It was always his method to keep well informed of anything going on at N.Y. That way, you could guard your job against any dangers.

He came up to the old mansion house quietly, through the rhododendrons and along the side of the building. As he turned a corner to stand outside the windows, he found Teddy Hooson already there, listening intently. Teddy started at his approach and then grinned. He gestured to Seth to keep quiet.

'What's this, then?' Seth whispered.

'There's a war on in there,' Teddy replied with his lips almost against Seth's ear.

And there was indeed.

'If it was owt to do with the spray from Emmerdale,' Joe was saying, with emphasis but still without anger, 'they'd have had the same trouble there, wouldn't they? It'd be showing by now because it was at least two days ago they got their supply and used it.'

'Are you sure they used it, and not the stuff we lent them?' Turner rejoined, very stiff.

'I'll ring them and find out, shall I?'

Turner pushed the phone at him without speaking. Reining in his annoyance at being treated this way, Joe dialled for Emmerdale. While he waited to be connected, Seth said quietly to Teddy, 'What's up then?'

'Joe just got back from the lab in Connelton. They spuds have been sprayed wi' Paraquat instead of di-meth.'

Seth gave Teddy a look, not entirely favourable. There was glee on the lad's face.

Joe got through to Emmerdale. He asked for Matt, but

Dolly told him Matt had taken some time off.

'Jack there then?'

'Nay, he's up top looking at the sheep.'

'Listen, Dolly – they sprayed the barley, didn't they?'

Dolly thought about it. 'I think they did, Joe, yes. Matt had that gear out.'

'Any trouble with it?'

'The gear?'

'No, the barley.'

'Oh. Not that I heard, Joe. Why?'

'Nothing, never mind. Only, ask Matt to get in touch when he gets back, eh? It's important.' Joe put back the receiver and looked at Turner. 'Only Dolly there. She's got no idea what they've used, of course. We'll have to wait for Matt or Jack.'

Turner was leaning back in his swivel chair behind the desk, moving restlessly as if marshalling facts in his head. Joe said, rather carefully, 'There is one obvious explanation, you know. That Hooson made a mistake, filled the sprayer with Paraquat in mistake for di-meth.'

Seth was secretly amused to feel Hooson stiffen at the suggestion. But he need not have worried, for Alan Turner sprang to his defence.

'I know you don't think highly –'

'It's not that, Alan. But mistakes do happen.'

'I can't believe that. The drums are clearly marked.'

'Yet it *has* happened. It's either a mistake or deliberate.'

'*What?*'

'There's no alternative. Mistake or deliberate.'

'You're not suggesting Hooson –'

Joe muttered something the eavesdroppers didn't quite hear. 'What did you say?' Turner demanded.

'I said, I'm not suggesting anything. I just want to get to the bottom of it.'

'There's something we've forgotten!' Turner exclaimed.

'What's that?'

'The broken hasp on the door of the shed, Joe! Someone could have got in there to make mischief.'

'Not a tramp, you mean?'

'That's just what I mean.'

'But why?'

'I don't know. But I intend to find out – I want a good look at those bottles, Joe. Come on!'

The eavesdroppers removed themselves hastily, since to get to the Land-Rover Alan Turner and Joe would probably come along the path to the front of the house.

Seth caught Hooson by the arm as they were about to separate. 'What you been up to?'

'Me? I done nothing! All I did was use the stuff,' Teddy said in a tone of injured virtue.

'Up on forty acre, was it? I think I'll go and take a look.' As they parted, Seth flung a last remark over his shoulder. '*You'd* best get ready for the inquisition, my lad!'

But Teddy went his own way in the full confidence of not being in any trouble.

At the store-shed, Joe followed Turner in. 'You're not suggesting someone got in here deliberately, to ruin our potato crop?' he was saying as Turner began to sort out empty containers from full.

'You said yourself – deliberate or accident. And now I've taken a second look at that broken hasp, I'm inclined to go for deliberate!'

As he finished speaking, he picked up the bottle, now empty, which had contained di-methoate returned by Emmerdale Farm. 'Try this one,' he commanded.

'It's one of those from Emmerdale –'

'Just try it!' Turner exclaimed.

Joe took off the cap, tipped the bottle, and let some remains of liquid trickle out into an old tin lid. He bent to sniff at it. The unmistakably sharp odour of Paraquat came up to him.

'It's Paraquat,' he said, unable to believe it. He took up the other bottle that had come from Emmerdale and likewise tipped the remains of liquid towards its neck. Paraquat . . . 'It doesn't make sense,' he muttered.

Turner was watching, his brow furrowed in thought. He picked up a container labelled Paraquat. 'Let's take a look at this one.'

'But that *is* Paraquat –'

'Let's see.' They unscrewed the cap. Joe sniffed. 'Well?' demanded Turner.

Joe looked up at him blankly over the container. 'It's di-methoate.'

Turner nodded.

'What the heck's been going on?' Joe said.

'It's perfectly obvious. Someone has done a switch. That bloody field has been sprayed with weedkiller instead of aphid spray.'

'But . . . who'd want to do a thing like that?'

Alan Turner pursed his lips. He said in an icy tone: 'Someone who doesn't like the idea of farmers using weedkillers? Or someone who's got a grudge against N.Y. Estates?' He paused. 'Who do you think it might be, Joe? Who?'

'How the blazes should I know?' Joe retorted.

'Well, just think about it a moment.' Turner pointed. 'Those containers that had the Paraquat in them are from Emmerdale.'

Chapter Eight

Matt had sought out Henry in the back room of the Woolpack. Amos had been asked if he would leave them for a private conversation and because he respected and liked Matt more than most, he had not demurred.

Matt had laid his problem before Henry, with complete frankness. 'It's not that I want to leave Emmerdale, Henry,' he said.

'No, I'm sure of that.'

'Nor am I saying I've had a raw deal, or owt of that kind. But if I'm honest, I have to say I think Dolly feels that. And I have to think of Dolly.'

Henry was nodding in agreement. What he had heard had taken his breath away at first, but he had regained control of his thinking by now. When he heard Matt explain things, so simply and uncomplainingly, he was amazed at how obtuse they had all been. And how much they had taken Matt for granted!

They had been almost certain Matt would never move away from Emmerdale for a job. Because of that, they hadn't bestirred themselves on his behalf. Henry realized now, with shame, that if he had put himself out before now, he could have found some cottage or little house and by private arrangement put it within Matt's range to rent.

He simply hadn't thought of it. He had had most of his attention on Jack, who was somehow always in the centre of the stage. Jack needed money to do this or that, and because it meant a quiet life, they had given in. Then when Jack looked as if he might pack in the whole farming idea when he couldn't get his own way over organic methods for Hathersage, Henry had supplied that money out of his own funds.

He saw now that that money should have been spent on Matt.

'Y'see,' Matt said, 'I don't reckon this baby will be the only one. I think Dolly would like a family, a proper family. So you can understand that she's set on a place of our own.'

'She has a right,' Henry acknowledged.

'Happen I wouldn't have bothered over it if she hadn't felt so strongly. I wanted you to know how things stood.'

'Well, I appreciate your frankness, Matt. Not as I'd expect anything else from you.' He gave the conversation a moment's consideration. 'It'll be a nasty shock for everyone if you leave. Especially Annie.'

Matt looked uncomfortable. 'She does know we're looking for somewhere else to live.'

'She knows – or senses – more than that, Matt. She's been right worried, but too sensitive to go asking you for facts. She was resigned to your living away from the farm, housing being a problem anywhere close . . . but leaving the farm to work for N.Y. Estates is summat quite different. You don't need me to tell you that.'

'I thought she'd know summat was in the air. Ma's no fool, Henry. That's why I felt I had to come to you *now* and get it in the open. I don't like the feel of going behind Ma's back. Not that I am, mind!' And Matt coloured at the thought. 'I have to be fair to everyone, and first of all to my own wife. You see that, don't you, Henry?'

'I do, indeed I do.' Once more Henry mentally kicked himself for the thoughtlessness of the past. 'But I want to be fair to Annie, you understand. It's no fault of hers that this situation has come up.' Unspoken was the thought that though he himself was to blame – because he should have seen all round the problem – to some extent Jack's thoughtlessness was the chief factor. Jack bringing a ready-made family of a wife and two children to a house where there was not enough room for them, and within a few days snatching at the idea of refurbishing the barn . . . And not relinquishing it when Matt explained he and Dolly had had the same thought weeks ago.

'The thing is, Henry . . . This isn't going to be solved without somebody getting a bit of a blow. At least, not the way I see it.'

'Aye,' said Henry. 'And in coming to me you wanted to do . . . what?'

'Well . . . lay it on the line, like.'

'You want my advice, is that it?'

'I was hoping you might have some other solution.'

'An ultimatum, is that it? Do summat or I'll leave Emmerdale?'

Matt looked at him in consternation. 'I wouldn't do a thing like that, Henry!'

'Nay, lad, I know that. I'm just putting it in the plainest terms. Because when you come down to it, that's what it comes to. You don't want to leave Emmerdale to get a house, but you will if you have to. That's a sort of ultimatum.'

'You might look at it that way, I suppose. As far as I'm concerned I'm asking if you can think of a way out.'

There was a knock on the door. Amos put an apologetic head round. 'I'm sorry to disturb you but can I go through to the bar? It's time I started getting a few things ready.'

'Aye, go on, Amos,' said Henry. Amos hurried through, as if he had imaginary hands over his ears so as not to hear their conversation.

Matt got up. 'It's time I got back any road. There's milking waiting.'

'So there is. And I reckon we've been twice round the wheatfield with it in any case. How urgent is this, Matt?'

'Well, it's urgent in one way and not in another. Alan Turner said he'd ring today some time, just to hear how I was thinking. But so far he's not, and when he does I reckon I can tell him it's still being thought on. On the other hand, Dolly is on tenterhooks. She'll want it settled because there's a lot to do if we're to be in Tolly's Farmhouse afore the baby's born.'

'She's right there. Moving into a new home is never as quick and easy as we imagine . . . Listen, Matt, leave this with me till I've had a chance to see what I can come up with.'

'Should I tell Ma, d'you think?'

Henry hesitated. 'Not yet. Leave it with me.'

'I'm only too glad to, Henry,' Matt said in heartfelt tones as he went out.

Amos heard him go: the snick of the lock on the back door was unmistakable. He longed to dash back into the kitchen and find out what had been going on. But honour prevented him. He'd promised Mr Wilks he wouldn't intervene.

Matt set off along the village High Street too deep in thought to notice young Jackie Merrick turning into Vicarage Lane. Jackie was on his way to ask for advice also. Seth had proved almost useless, too interested in his own acquisition of knowledge to give him a thoughtful opinion. On matters of truth and honesty, the vicar was the best guide.

Jackie quite liked the vicar. He guessed him to be shy and diffident with others. He'd worked hard at making the village disco a success, although its music and ambience were foreign to his nature.

Donald Hinton opened the door to him, and if he was surprised at his visitor he made no sign. 'Jackie! How nice! You're just in time for a cup of tea!'

'Nay, Mr Hinton, I –'

'Come in, come in. I've just made one for myself.' He led the boy into the drawing-room, set him in an armchair, and hastened to sit behind the tea-tray. He could sense the boy was on the verge of changing his mind about the visit. Once get him trapped with a cup of tea in his hands, and he'd stay.

'Are you settling in at Emmerdale?' he asked as he poured a second cup.

'It's all right,' Jackie said without enthusiasm.

'You find it very different from living in the caravan.' He offered the tea, pushed the sugar bowl towards him. 'Much more room for one thing.'

'There's not that much.' No, there wasn't. And as to being as free to play his transistor – quite the reverse. Mrs Sugden preferred that classical stuff, bits of opera and orchestras playing with lots of violins and things. The one time he'd switched on his transistor to hear Heavy Metal, everybody had looked at him as if he'd gone mad, so he'd gone outside and played it in the barn. But that was *less* comfortable than the caravan!

'I hear you'll have a completely new home when the barn is converted,' Mr Hinton said, almost as if tuning into his thoughts.

Jackie stirred his tea. He scarcely heard what the vicar said. 'D'you reckon,' he began, 'you ought to rat on a pal when you know . . . he's done summat wrong, and that someone else . . . someone else might get the blame?'

Mr Hinton drew in a careful breath. So that was it. A moral dilemma. How wrong the general public were in thinking the young simply didn't care about right and wrong . . . 'The obvious answer to that is yes, at first glance. And I don't like the word "rat". That implies betrayal, and doing right – whatever the circumstances – can never be a betrayal.'

'If you don't know the circumstances I don't see how you can say that,' the lad retorted.

'It does sound a bit presumptuous.' He held out a plate of biscuits. 'Help yourself.' To his inner amusement Jackie took one and put it, whole, into his mouth. Even in the midst of a moral dilemma, the young have healthy appetites. 'A very famous man,' he went on, 'not perhaps a good man but a famous man, which makes it more telling . . . Francis Bacon – have you ever heard of him?'

Jackie, his mouth full of biscuit, shook his head.

'Well, he wrote that truth is the sovereign good of human nature. Now if you accept that, as I do, it follows that however loyal a man may feel to a friend, truth is higher than that loyalty.' He picked up his own tea-cup and sipped. 'I take it that this case you are speaking of is a matter of a choice between truth and loyalty?'

110

Jackie thoughtfully picked up another biscuit, crunched for a moment, then said: 'If nobody asks you the questions, you don't have to give untruthful answers, do you?'

'Ah. Loyalty by silence, you mean? But then you would have to watch an innocent person suffer the consequence of your silence.'

There was a pause. Hinton did not push the issue.

Jackie said: 'What if the innocent person isn't so innocent in other respects and deserves to suffer a bit?'

Oh ho, thought Hinton, amazed. What subtlety! For the moment he took refuge in another quotation. 'Hamlet – in the play, you know? – he says, "Treat every man according to his deserts, and who shall 'scape whipping?" We're all less than innocent in some respect, Jackie.'

'Yeah . . . well . . .'

'If you were caught stealing a five pound note would you think it right if you were sent to prison for murder?'

'It's nothing like that –'

'I didn't suppose it was. But the principle is the same; as Hamlet said, who has the right to be judge and jury?'

Jackie took a long swig at his tea. It struck him that the tea was different from the kind served at Emmerdale: it had a sort of smoky taste, not bad for a change. The rest of his mind was struggling with his problem.

'Is it a very close friend that's involved?' the vicar asked at length.

Jackie was a little taken aback. 'I don't know as he's a friend at all, really. He's more . . . well, he's a sort of pal.'

'And the person who's likely to get the blame – he's not a pal?'

No he's not, thought Jackie. And that was where the trouble lay. If it had been somebody he cared as little about as Teddy Hooson, he'd have gone into the office at Home Farm and told what he knew. But because it was Jack Sugden . . . Truth is the sovereign good of human nature. The truth was, he half-wanted Jack Sugden to be landed right in it, as Hooson kept saying. Serve him right, big-headed know-it-all.

There wasn't much 'sovereign good' in feeling like that. Somehow talking to Mr Hinton made his own feelings seem . . . well . . . selfish and childish.

He bethought himself of the letter from his father – from Tom Merrick. 'I've been told,' he said, 'that you should always look after Number One because nobody else will.'

'Quite true.' A man's own soul is his first concern. 'It depends how you do it, doesn't it? You have to be able to live with yourself – that Number One you've been looking after. If you hurt other people, either with intention or by lack of action, you have to answer to yourself for it. I can't see how a man could be happy if he had allowed harm to befall when . . .'

He let it die away. He didn't want to say too much.

Jackie got up and set down his empty cup. 'Well, thanks for the tea.'

'A pleasure.' He followed the lad into the hall. 'Are you sure there's nothing more I can do for you?'

'No thanks. It's summat I have to sort out for myself.'

'Goodbye for the present then, Jackie.' As he closed the door he thought, I shall know soon, by what happens in the village, if I've handled that right.

Jackie gave a lot of thought to what the vicar had said. 'You have to be able to live with yourself . . .' He knew very well that Teddy could get the people at Emmerdale into a lot of trouble, and Joe Sugden too. Though he might tell himself he didn't give a rap over what happened to his stepfather, all the same he knew he could never be easy if he let the trouble fall on him and through him on Mrs Sugden, who didn't deserve it, and on Sam Pearson, who had been nice to him.

Next morning he and Seth put in three hours' hard work. Seth was talkative now and again, in his usual way. He was plotting how to get free beer from Amos Brearly. 'I'm going to give him a scoop for his paper,' he said.

'About what? What scoop?'

'About the disaster to the crops.'

'Hey,' said Jackie. 'Mr Turner told us not to let on about that.' Mr Turner had been round the farms soon after eight, warning his staff to keep their mouths shut.

'Nowt can be kept quiet long in Beckindale,' Seth said. 'That's why I want to get in quick wi' Amos, as soon as he opens this morning.'

He was packing up his gear to break off work, although

it was only just after ten. 'You going there now?'

'Aye. Coming along? Should be summat worth seeing – Amos Brearly giving away a free pint.'

'Nay, that's your idea of fun. I've got summat else to do.'

'Oh? What?' For Seth would have thought the lad would enjoy a joke against Amos, who treated him as if he had no right to come into the pub although he was now of age.

'I'm off to see Teddy.'

At once Seth was all agog. 'What about?'

'It's a private matter, Seth,' Jackie said with some formality.

Private matter? Happen summat to do with Jackie's sister Sandie, who seemed to have a right crush on that lad Teddy. 'I wouldn't trust him if I was you!' he called as Jackie walked away.

Perhaps that was Jackie's opinion too. He waved a hand at Seth and went on.

Teddy Hooson was cleaning the tractor in a private lane next to Long Meadow field on N.Y.'s land. Jackie came up behind him without being heard, and touched him on the shoulder. Teddy leaped about a foot into the air, symptomatic of edginess.

'Thought I was the cops, did you?' Jackie enquired.

'Oh, it's you! What's the idea, creeping up behind me like that? Nearly gave mc heart failure.'

'Guilty conscience?'

'You what? I've nowt to feel guilty about.'

'Come off it, Teddy. Only the other day you were boasting how you were going to land the Sugdens right in it, and now almost the minute after, Joe Sugden's being blamed for somehow letting the potato crop be spoiled and it's summat to do with chemicals returned by Emmerdale.'

'Ho! You know a lot, don't you?'

'Only what I've heard. But Peters was brought in at crack of dawn today to put a new lock on the chemicals shed, and told us the padlock hasp had been damaged. Mr Turner's going round saying no one's to say a word about the wrong chemicals being used on the spuds—'

'Well, it'd be bad publicity, wouldn't it? Rank inefficiency, letting harmful chemicals be mixed up with good ones.'

'I reckon it was you mixed 'em up, Teddy,' Jackie said.

'Well, that's no secret. But everybody knows it wasn't my fault. Somebody'd put Paraquat in the di-meth containers.'

'Yeh,' Jackie agreed, 'and that somebody was you.'

'Eh?' Teddy was highly indignant. 'You're off your chop! I don't know what you're talking about!'

'You know well enough. You haven't got cloth ears.'

'I hear you talking rubbish!'

'It isn't rubbish. You deliberately sprayed that forty acres with Paraquat, and you're working it now so that Jack Sugden'll get the blame.'

'Ha,' sneered Teddy, a bit taken aback by Jackie's earnestness, 'you want to be the loving son saving your stepdad from disgrace, is that it? Get a hug and a kiss from your Ma?'

Jackie refused to be diverted into anger. 'You told me you were going to fix him 'cos he made you look small in front of Sandie.'

'Nobody makes me look small, mate,' Teddy interrupted.

'Oh yes they do. Joe Sugden took the rug out from under your feet when he sacked you. You really felt a fool over that.'

'Oh, dry your eyes! I fixed him, didn't I? Turner reinstated me.'

'But that wasn't what you wanted. You wanted an apology from Joe – and you can't stand to remember you didn't get it.'

'I'm not saying I love any of 'em. All I'm saying is, you're talking through your hat.'

'No I'm not. I can prove you did it.'

That stopped Teddy dead. He gave the other lad a hard stare. Then he said: 'All I did was spray them spuds with di-meth as instructed by Joe Sugden. If there weren't di-meth in the bottles he told me to use, that's nothing to do with me!'

'Oh yes it is. You switched 'em.'

'Don't be so bloody daft!'

'You did, Teddy, I know you did.'

'How? How do you know? Eh? There was di-meth

returned from Emmerdale, weren't there? By your stepdad – and everybody knows he don't love N.Y. If you ask me, he was getting his own back for that careless spraying by the helicopter as caused him to lose two cows.'

'Teddy, he got compensation for that.'

'What's that matter? He's one of them eco-freaks, isn't he? Wants to keep everything pure and non-toxic. Like he wants to keep your sister pure.'

'Leave her out of it!' Jackie shouted, suddenly in a flare of temper.

'But he can't, can he? Your stepdad – your real dad – he's got to be careful wi' Sandie because he knows how easy it was to get your ma in the family way!'

Jackie threw himself on Teddy with hands reaching for his throat. Teddy had wanted physical rough-stuff, to put an end to the cross-questioning that was getting too close to the truth. But he hadn't bargained for Jackie's furious strength.

He was struggling for air. At first he clawed at Jackie's hands, but then instinctive cunning took over. He brought his knee up hard into Jackie's stomach. Gasping, Jackie fell back.

Teddy was on him in a moment, throwing punches to the head and the neck. Jackie went over backwards. He lunged out with his arms, cut Teddy's legs from under him, and they were rolling around in the lane, one on top and then the other.

Stones from the wall dug into them as they wrestled to and fro. Dust streaked their faces. Teddy got hold of a broken hawthorn twig and made a stab at Jackie's eyes. Jackie rolled free, got up, and kicked out with his heavily-booted foot. It caught Teddy in the ribs as he was getting up. Over he went, clutching himself round the ribcage. But he came up from his knees ready to butt Jackie in the face.

Jackie darted aside. The other boy went staggering into the dry ditch. He sprawled into it, slithering upside down further and further into the hollow, nettles and brambles catching at him.

Jackie stooped over, breathing hard, glaring at him. The other lad looked comic, arms and legs forced up in the air like a landed crab, his rear nicely wedged in the ditch.

'Ha,' Jackie gasped, trying to laugh, 'pity there's no water in it, you'd be in among the slime where you belong, Teddy Hooson!'

With that he turned and staggered off in a half-trot, already half-ashamed of the outburst of violence. What was the use of coming to blows with a twerp like Teddy Hooson? You couldn't beat any decency into him whatever you did.

But first things first. He had to get to Seth's hidey-hole and tidy himself up before anybody saw him and started a parliamentary enquiry. It was just his bad luck to cross the road as Joe Sugden came round the lane in the Home Farm Land-Rover.

Joe drew up with a slam of the brakes. Jackie vaulted the wall into the next field and took cover in a hollow where there was a dew pond.

'Jackie!' cried Joe, half-leaning out of the driving seat. 'Jackie? What's up?'

But there was no answer, and he didn't quite know where the boy had got to. Frowning in concern, Joe got back in and drove on.

His aim was to oversee Teddy Hooson. Although not required to give him orders, Joe was expected to see the work done. He saw the top of the tractor cabin and remarked to himself with some grimness that it was still in Long Meadow lane where it had been last time he went by an hour ago. What the blazes was the young fool doing *now*?

What he was doing was sitting on the verge of the lane, dabbing at a cut on his face with a grubby shirt tail.

'What the heck!' cried Joe, getting out of the Land-Rover to survey him. 'What's been going on?'

'Mind your own business!' growled Teddy, flinching as he cleared grit from his cut.

'You been fighting with Jackie?'

'No, I been having ten rounds wi' Mohammad Ali. So what?'

'So what the blazes are you up to? You're both supposed to be working – '

'I'll be working again in a minute, soon's I get my face to function again.'

116

'What's it all about? I need to know.'

'And I don't need to tell you.' Teddy got up to his feet with much wincing, but faced Joe. 'Gonna sack me?'

'Now, listen, Teddy,' Joe began with considerable forbearance.

'You Sugdens!' Teddy suddenly blurted. 'Bloody pests, the lot of you!' He spat forcibly on the ground at Joe's feet.

'Teddy, this is doing you no good –'

'Drop dead!' Teddy shouted, and ran through the nearest gap in the wall into the field on the far side of the lane.

Joe stood watching him go. No sense in going after him. Besides, he had other calls to make round the estate. But it was dead peculiar, no doubt about it.

Jackie, diverted from the track he'd meant to take that would bring him in through the lower part of Verney Wood to Home Farm, came out above the High Street of Beckindale. He didn't want to go through the village.

He came down through the churchyard, staying out of sight behind the gravestones and in among the cypress and yew. Donald Hinton, coming out of the church after making it ready for a christening, saw the lurking figure. For a moment he was startled, then recognized it.

'Jackie!'

The boy turned, all ready for flight.

His face was a mess. He had a bruise which was going to turn into a black eye, a cut on his forehead that was bleeding quite profusely, a lot of dirt on his face and clothes, and a general appearance of having been in the wars.

'Jackie! Where are you going?'

Jackie said the first word that came into his head. 'Home!'

He meant the caravan, where he could be private. Hinton took it that he meant Emmerdale. 'Good heavens, lad, think of the shock it'll be to your mother if she sees you like this! Come with me into the vicarage and clean up a bit.'

'Well . . . I . . .'

'Come along.' Hinton took him firmly by the elbow,

knowing that of course if Jackie took to his heels he had no way of stopping him. 'You don't have to tell me what happened,' he said, talking so as to hold the boy's attention. 'I don't need to know the ins and outs, but you ought to get that cut washed otherwise who knows, it may turn nasty. I've some sticky plaster in the First Aid box.'

'Yeh . . . well . . . thanks . . .'

Hinton took him in through the back door of the vicarage, directly into the kitchen. He sat him in a chair, switched on the electric kettle for boiled water, and went in search of the First Aid box.

As he was on his way back to the kitchen his front door bell rang. He went into the kitchen, gave the box to Jackie. 'Find the biggest packet of sticky plaster. I'll be back in a minute to wash the cut.'

He then went to the door. To his consternation, Jack Sugden, the boy's father, was standing on the doorstep.

'Did I just see you take Jackie through the churchyard into the house?' he demanded.

'Oh . . . yes . . . in fact.'

'He looked as if he'd been roughed up. What's happened?'

Hinton hesitated. 'You'd better come in,' he invited, and stood aside. He indicated the kitchen. 'In there.'

Jack strode in. Hinton saw the look of astonished resentment that came over the boy's face when he saw him. He turned his eyes in reproach towards the vicar, who said quickly, 'I just happened on Jackie and thought he needed a little first aid.'

'Been in a fight, has he? What about?'

Hinton said in reproof, 'In my profession we try to help first, asking questions afterwards.'

'That's all very well,' Jack said in annoyance, thinking of Tom Merrick and the way he'd probably brought up the boy, 'but we can't have fisticuffs over nothing. What have you been up to?'

Had he asked with kindness, Jackie would have blurted it all out. But the tone of voice brought its own reward. 'Mind your own business,' Jackie said.

'It *is* my business.'

'Since when?'

'Since I have some feeling for your mother, which you apparently haven't –'

'Leave Mum out of this!' cried Jackie.

'You can't leave her out! When are you going to grow up and realize that? What you do affects her.'

Jackie leapt to his feet. 'You can tell me how to behave when you know how to behave yourself!' he shouted.

'Now look here, Jackie –'

Hinton intervened. 'That will do, I think!' he said, with a sharpness that silenced them both. 'If you have no respect for each other, please show some for my home. I will not have it used as a cockpit!'

Jack drew back. He was accustomed to thinking of Donald Hinton as ineffectual. 'Sorry, vicar,' he muttered. 'I got a bit carried away. But his mother gets upset.'

'She's no reason to be upset over this unless you tell her!' Jackie interrupted.

'Well, of course I won't . . . But you ought to know better than –'

'How do you know if it was my fault?' the boy challenged.

'Well . . . then tell me . . .'

Jackie made no reply. Mr Hinton made a little movement of concern as the blood began flowing again over the cut.

'Would you like to put the plaster on now, vicar?' Jackie said.

He did so, unexpectedly expert. He stood between father and son, doing his best to protect the boy from the criticism implicit in every line of Jack Sugden's attitude.

'Are you going to give me an explanation?' Jack demanded.

'No,' Jackie said calmly, 'I'm not. I'm telling you nothing, ever. And you know why? Because you think you know all the answers. Well, you can get what satisfaction you can out of them.'

'Jackie!' Hinton warned. He could not stand by and allow disrespect from a son to his father.

'Sorry, sir,' Jackie said, and lapsed into silence.

Jack turned to Hinton as if towards an ally. But Hinton did not respond. 'I had a chat with Jackie the other day,'

119

he said, coming at the problem obliquely, 'and we talked about Bacon. Francis Bacon – you'll be familiar with his works?'

'A little,' Jack said in surprise.

'You'll know his remark about jesting Pilate, then.'

'Well . . . yes . . .'

'He had the right idea, don't you think?'

Jack met his quiet gaze. *What is Truth, said jesting Pilate, and would not stay for an answer.* It was a hint if ever there was one. He had definitely outstayed his welcome. The vicar, of course, would never turn him out of doors – certainly not in front of Jackie – but he had been told to make himself scarce.

Going a little red under his dark skin, Jack turned for the door. 'I'm sorry, Jackie,' he said. 'I shouldn't have got at you. We'll try and sort it out later. Goodbye, vicar – don't see me out, I know my way.'

With that he was gone. Jackie heard the front door close behind him. He blew out a breath of relief. Then he grinned with sudden boyishness at Mr Hinton. 'You got rid of him, didn't you? That was a ticking-off you meant.'

'Not quite – it was a suggestion. I thought you were both too heated to go on with the conversation at the moment.' Hinton found a packet of new kitchen cloths and gave one to Jackie to bathe the dirt off his face. 'I'll leave you to it,' he said. 'I generally have a glass of pre-lunch sherry about now – when you're tidied up, perhaps you'd like to join me for one?'

Jackie was astounded at being treated in this grown-up style. He was suddenly overcome with self-consciousness. 'Oh, I . . .'

'It's much nicer to drink in company,' urged Hinton.

'Oh well then, thanks.'

Hinton smiled and went to the drawing-room. He had poured two glasses and put them on his good silver tray when Jackie reappeared. 'Cheers,' he said, picking up his glass.

'Cheers,' said Jackie, taking a tentative sip. He found the drink unexpectedly pleasant. One thing you could say about the vicar – he had nice things around him.

'I did . . . did have a good reason for getting in a fight,'

120

he said.

'I didn't doubt it. And another thing I don't doubt is that it had something to do with what we talked about. You remember, we agreed that Truth was the sovereign good. But Truth is difficult to face, Jackie. Sometimes something that is truly good blazes with a light that hurts our eyes. Jack looks at truth, in his own way, and if he is sometimes a little blind, it's because the light is too intense for him.'

'Hm,' said Jackie, feeling a pleasant warmth flowing through him from the sherry. 'Is that a way of telling me to tell the truth?'

'I have no reason to think you are not telling the truth. I don't think you are an untruthful person. But I want you to try to see Jack's point of view. And perhaps that includes not *hiding* the truth from him.'

Jackie gave the matter a long moment of careful thought. 'I've decided,' he said, 'it's not right to hide it. But I'm not telling it to him.' Unspoken was the thought, 'I'd rather die than justify myself to him!' Hinton sat looking at him without criticism. 'I'll tell *you*,' said Jackie, 'and you can tell him.'

Jack Sugden would have been dismayed if he knew that his hasty intervention had only succeeded in driving yet another wedge between himself and his son.

Chapter Nine

Seth Armstrong was into the Woolpack almost in front of Old Walter when Amos Brearly opened the doors for morning trading. Amos practically backed away from him. He knew Seth liked his pint, but this unseemly haste was overdoing it.

But once he reached the bar, Seth seemed in no hurry. 'Morning, Amos,' he said with amiability. 'Nice morning, ain't it?'

'It has been so far,' Amos said, as he pulled Walter's first pint.

'And I could tell you summat as would make it nicer.'

'Fancy that. I s'pose you came in here to order a drink,

though, not to make my day brighter?'

'My order's the usual,' Seth said in a lordly manner. He watched Amos pull the handle. 'Had any good scoops lately?'

Amos filled the tankard, set it on the bar top, and waited. Seth too waited. 'That'll be sixty-eight, please, Seth.'

'What if I told you I could give you a scoop in return for a couple of those?' Seth jerked his head at his beer.

'I'd say I'd rather have the money, thank you, Seth Armstrong.'

'Eeh!' sighed Seth. 'You've no ambition, that's your problem. Don't you want a scoop that'd make the nationals?'

Amos was tempted. But experience with Seth had taught him never to count any chickens before the eggs were laid. 'As if you'd know what'd make the nationals,' he temporized.

'What d'you mean! I read the papers, don't I? I know what goes in the headlines! "Crop Poisoned! Nation's Food Sabotaged In Beckindale!"' Seth had leaned forward to give this sample in a breathy undertone. He straightened, smiling smugly. 'How about that, then?'

Despite all his experience, Amos was weakening. 'This "sabotage" happened on N.Y. Estates?'

Seth made no response. He tapped his tankard suggestively. Amos gave in.

'All right . . . But you only get the other pint if the story's any good.'

Seth grinned to himself. He'd spin it out to be worth more than two pints, or his name wasn't Seth Armstrong. He leaned across the bar and began his saga in a quiet, dramatic tone.

Luckily Alan Turner was quite unaware of this. Native caution had caused him to go the rounds this morning warning his men against gossip. After much delay in the long distance network he had at last got through to Spalding on the phone. There he had spoken with the director of the Scientific Division who had told him in explicit terms to keep his own mouth shut.

'Shouldn't I report it to the police, though?' he

countered. 'I mean, malicious damage – '

'On no account!' Walden interrupted. 'Do you want it to come to court? We'd be reported by the press, and what would the report say? That we were so careless with our chemicals that we ruined an entire crop of potatoes, that we let unauthorized persons have access to the store-shed, that there's some nutcase with such a deep grudge against N.Y. that he substitutes weedkiller for aphid spray . . .'

'Oh, I see. I never thought of that.'

'The next question a reporter wants answered is, Why should anyone have a deep grudge against N.Y.? And then old scores are revived, and we look a bunch of villains if not idiots.'

'I see, Walden, I quite see your point. Rely on me. I won't say a word to the police.'

Joe had been privy to Turner's end of the conversation. 'Does that mean,' he said indignantly, 'that whoever did this is going to get away with it?'

Turner gave him a look that might have said, As it's very likely your own brother who did it, it's lucky for you it's being kept quiet. Aloud he said, 'There's to be no publicity, absolutely none. And I see their point. The whole thing is a gift to the natural-food lobby.'

'Aye?'

'And that's lucky for us, my son,' Turner said, with something of a grin.

'I can't see how?'

'It means they can't afford to sack us! They know damn well I'd bring suit if they tried that, and it would all come out. No, they're stuck with us, they have to look after us to keep us quiet.'

Joe gave him a stare of utter disbelief and distaste. Turner laughed.

'Oh, you're such an innocent! I told you once, big business exists on the basis of quid pro quo. Well, in this instance, the quid is our silence and the quo is N.Y.'s good name. And somewhere in there our jobs are neatly safeguarded.'

'And the crop? What about that?'

'Oh, we'll lose it, of course. Nothing to be done about it. We'll have to write it off on the books. But I expect Head

Office thinks it's cheap at the price. No bad publicity, and no complaints from the big chemical firms about our bringing shame on them – firms like that prefer peace and quiet about their products.' Turner had decided it was an occasion for a little celebration. After twenty-four very bad hours, he had managed to survive very nicely, thank you. He produced the whisky bottle and two glasses from the sideboard. 'Have a drop?'

Joe nodded. He too felt in need of a little stiffener. He'd been really worried about the whole affair. He had foreseen a law suit, Jack in court declaiming about the wickedness of agro-business, and the lord knows what else.

He was satisfied in his own mind that Jack had nothing to do with the ruination of the potatoes. He understood it was a deliberate act, however, and his favourite suspect was Teddy Hooson. But he had learned enough about business diplomacy to know he mustn't mention that to Turner. Turner had no particular liking or interest in Teddy Hooson, but he'd defend him because Hooson was a trouble-maker and the last thing Turner wanted was trouble.

All the same . . . 'You reckon my brother Jack had summat to do with it?' he murmured as he accepted the scotch from Turner.

'I never said that!' his boss said at once.

'Well, let's say you thought it to yourself. Did you mention that to Walden – that it was deliberate and you suspected one particular person?'

'I had to say it was deliberate, Joe. That was to cover *ourselves*! We couldn't be thought guilty of negligence, now could we. But as to naming names . . .' He took a sip of his drink and then said in a friendly tone, 'Let me clue you in, my son. We could never prove this was done deliberately, and Head Office see that. But even if we could, same argument applies. If a loony can switch chemicals that easily, it means it can be done again. They don't want that idea gaining ground.'

Joe accepted that and thought it over. By God, where did truth and justice come in? Keep it quiet, never mind who did what, draw a pretty veil over it . . . He was nerving himself to mention Hooson when the phone rang.

Turner was nearest. He picked it up. He listened after announcing himself, and his broad face darkened. 'Who told you this rigmarole, Amos?' he demanded.

Joe sat up. Turner raised his shoulders in a shrug of annoyance, but forced joviality into his voice. 'Of course I understand about the confidentiality of a reporter's sources . . . Yes . . . yes . . . Whoever it is, you should . . . Well, so you say, Amos, but I'm afraid you've been having your leg pulled.'

'What's he found out?' Joe asked.

Turner waved at him to be quiet. 'There's no truth in it whatever. Absolutely none, I assure you. N.Y. take much greater care of their crops than that.'

Thinly over the phone, Joe could hear Amos's voice protesting.

'If you publish, I shall get N.Y. to bring an action for libel . . . Of course we would, why not? We can't have our good name . . . Yes . . . Well, I should have thought you were too clever to be taken in by malicious gossip, Amos!'

He listened a moment more, said goodbye, and slammed back the receiver. 'Have you said anything to anyone about this?' he demanded of Joe.

'Don't be daft,' said he.

'Well, I've said nothing, I've warned the men to say nothing, and only Head Office knows otherwise. So who's been blabbing to Amos Brearly?'

Joe thought. 'I suppose . . . anyone who wants to do us more damage. In other words . . .'

Turner took up the thought. 'The person who did it in the first place.'

This wasn't a comforting idea. They could of course control their own people, but they couldn't control the villain of the piece. Whoever he may be, Joe added to that in his mind. And it certainly isn't Jack, because Jack's too fond of Amos to drag him into a thing like this.

But for the moment there was nothing to be done. For all his oddities, Amos wasn't the type to give away the name of his informant: strange though his views on journalism might be, he would stand by the code of ethics that protected his source.

It was to be hoped they had squelched speculation. All

they could do now was wait and see.

Turner had been delayed in getting started on his day's work by the problems of getting through to Spalding and having a confidential conversation. Now he had letters to give Pat Merrick for typing up. Joe took his departure: Turner tried to catch up with his work. As time came round for lunch, Turner gave final instructions to Pat.

'I have to go to a business lunch in Harrogate,' he explained. 'When you've typed those, give them to Joe to sign. And if he wants me, I'll be in Harrogate until late tonight.'

'Yes, I understand.'

Turner was putting papers in his briefcase. For once he was unwilling to set off on a round of business conviviality. 'Listen, Pat, if anyone . . . anyone at all . . . asks if there's been any trouble of any kind at N.Y., say you don't know what they're talking about – understand?'

'Well, yes,' said Pat, who didn't understand at all.

He saw he'd have to explain a little. 'There's a silly story going round that there's been some sort of accident here, but it's all rubbish, total rubbish, and we want it scotched . . .'

'Oh, I see.' She took it completely at face value. 'Anything else, Mr Turner?'

'No, I don't think – ' He broke off, snapping his fingers. 'If Matt Skilbeck rings, tell him I'll be in touch. One or two things have prevented me from following up something with him, but I'll see to it the minute I'm back. Okay?'

'Yes, okay.'

Turner nodded and hurried out to his car. He was only just going to make it in time to Harrogate, and that was a nuisance because he liked to be there first, settled with a drink and able to ask his colleague what he was having, thus putting him under an obligation from the outset.

Pat picked up the notes he had left for his letters. With them was a small collection of other papers, which she supposed she was to file. She picked them up, separated them from the letters, and was about to put them in alphabetical order when a name caught her eye – a name that Turner had just mentioned.

126

Matt Skilbeck . . .

She put the papers down, carried the notes to the typewriter, and typed the first two letters. Then a glance at her watch told her it was time to go to the Woolpack to meet Jack, who had arranged to have a pub lunch there with her.

He was seated at a table in a corner, with a half of bitter at his elbow. He was reading the newspaper. She touched his arm. He at once got up to pull out a chair for her, kissed her lightly on the cheek, and debated with himself whether to tell her about the scene with young Jackie in the vicarage. But first he had to get her her lunch.

'What are you having, Pat?'

'Can I have bread and cheese and a tomato juice?'

Amos, who seemed to be in sole charge this lunchtime, gave him the tomato juice and said he would bring over two bread-and-cheese in a minute. Jack sat down beside Pat. 'Jack,' she plunged in, 'I've got something serious to tell you.'

Oh lord, he thought. She's heard about Jackie and the fight.

Nothing of the kind. 'I was going to file some papers at the office this morning,' she said, in a half-whisper, 'and there was a memo from Head Office to Mr Turner saying it was in order to take on Matt Skilbeck as shepherd.'

'What!'

'Has Matt said anything?'

Jack had to take a moment before replying. 'Not a word,' he admitted, although he could hardly believe Matt would be so deceitful.

'I thought you ought to know.' She shook her tawny head. 'Terrible, isn't it?'

'Does Joe know?' Jack asked, his mind moving quickly through all the ramifications.

'He must, mustn't he? It's Joe who supervises the actual work force. Mr Turner would never go about hiring anyone without asking Joe.'

Her husband sat back in his chair. His face was a picture: disbelief, resentment, indignation . . . He was about to speak but held his peace when Amos appeared behind Pat with two plates. 'There you are,' said he, 'as fine a piece of Wensleydale as you'll get anywhere, if I do say so myself.' He hovered, watching them unwrap knife and fork from the paper napkins.

'We've got all we want, thanks, Amos,' Jack said, anxious to be rid of him so as to finish questioning Pat about the memo.

'Er . . . I was wondering . . . you being a fellow author, Jack . . .'

'Yes?' He tried not to show his impatience. Poor old Amos, he was harmless.

'If somebody sells you a news item, and you find out after that it was a leg-pull, can you claim back the price you paid? I mean, in your experience in London and everywhere, did you meet reporters who had that kind of problem?'

'Nay, can't say as I did, Amos. And I'd say that you just have to claim the money back as expenses from the paper, and write it off as experience.'

'Oh . . . aye . . . I suppose I could claim the money . . . Aye . . . All t'same, ought I to verify first whether it's really a leg-pull?'

'That's up to you. Whichever it is, you're still entitled to claim expenses.'

'So I am,' Amos said, much cheered, and removed himself.

'What was all that about?' Pat asked.

'Search me. Listen, Pat, did you get the impression Matt had agreed to take this shepherding job?'

'I didn't see owt about that. Mr Turner did say to me as he would follow something up with Matt when he got back from Harrogate.'

'Harrogate? When's he back?'

'Late tonight or tomorrow morning, I gather. He said to tell Joe he could be reached there.'

'Aye,' Jack said bitterly, 'Joe's probably to ring him when he's got Matt nicely rounded up! Well, it's not on! I'm going to get home right this minute and have it out with Matt.'

'Jack!' She caught his arm as he rose. 'You can't do that! That paper I saw was confidential, between Turner and Head Office, to do wi' Matt. You can't go barging –'

'Oh, can't I!'

'But . . .' She refused to let go his sleeve. 'Sit down, eat your food. Think a bit before you go rushing in, love.'

There was just enough of the echo of the old saying, Fools rush in, to make Jack pause. He sat down again. 'Aye,' he said with a bitter sigh, 'I suppose it'd be a shame to waste this good piece of Wensleydale . . .'

Chapter Ten

It hadn't occurred to Jack to wonder why Amos was handling the midday trade alone at the Woolpack. There was a good reason, one which concerned Jack himself, though he would have been surprised to hear it.

Henry Wilks was at Emmerdale Farm, conducting a mini-conference. It had all come about informally: Henry had gone to Annie for coffee. He then waited until Matt had gone back to his work, Dolly had taken the bus to Hotten in search of baby knitting-wool, and Sam had gone to his vegetable plot to fetch lettuce and spring onions for the midday meal.

When the kitchen had thus emptied itself, Annie smiled faintly. 'Well, we're private enough now, Henry . . .'

'Aye.' He sipped a second cup of coffee, trying to get his thoughts in order.

'It's about what Matt said when he came to see you?'

'He asked my advice.'

'And what advice did you give him?'

'I'd none to give. In fact, lass, I'm here to ask you.'

'I haven't any either,' she confessed. Her angular face, usually so composed, had lines of worry today. 'All I know is, I'm going to do all I can to keep Matt working here.'

Henry gave a little snort of laughter. 'Well, I'm with you there!'

She rose to take a tray of cakes out of the oven. 'Will it put you out if I deal with these, Henry?'

'Not a bit. I know you have your work to do. I've mine, too, but Amos has been surprisingly amenable about letting me take myself off. I think he senses it's something serious, and to do with Matt.'

129

'Aye,' Annie said, tipping little cakes out of the tray, 'Amos thinks a lot of Matt.'

'So do we all, Annie!'

She said with a sigh, 'But how often do we show it?'

Neither spoke for a long moment. Annie put the little cakes on a wire tray to cool and fetched out another batch from the oven.

'I blame myself,' Henry said at last. 'I'm supposed to know something about management, but it never occurred to me to think of Matt as a management problem.'

'A problem? He's never a problem, Henry.'

'But he *is*! That's what we've got to recognize. He has his rights like everybody else but we've never bothered to see that, and now it's become a problem. It serves us right for not doing anything about it afore this.'

Annie's back was to him as she busied herself with the baking. But she nodded. 'We've got to sort it,' she said. 'I can't let Matt leave Emmerdale –'

'He doesn't want to, lass!'

'That's just what I was going to say, Henry – he's being forced by circumstances to take a step that's really against his nature.'

'You don't think he's being forced by . . . Dolly?'

'Henry!' She whirled on him. 'Never say that! Never say a word against Dolly in my presence! Dolly doesn't want to go any more than Matt does, I'll stake my life on that. But fair's fair – she has her rights, just as Matt has.'

'What can he do, Annie? She's expecting a baby, it's only natural she wants a place of her own. In fact, the marvel is that she's never got insistent about it afore now.' Henry hesitated. 'I think having Jack's family here has brought it to a head.'

Annie knew Henry would do almost anything to avoid blaming Jack or, through Jack, herself. But she had to acknowledge inwardly that a kind of selfishness had made her blind to the needs of others. She had wanted her eldest son to bring his wife to Emmerdale: that was only right and fitting. So of course Pat's children had to come too, and she had not only agreed to that but willed it to be so, because she longed to have her grandson here at the farm.

She never asked herself if she would have been so

insistent if both Pat's children had been by Tom Merrick. She was sure in her own mind that she was as fond of Sandie as she was of Jackie. Yet would it have been so imperative, before the wedding, to persuade herself that they could find room for everybody – if Jackie had not been her true grandson?

She banished these thoughts by saying, 'That problem will solve itself when Jack and his family will be in the barn.'

Henry got to his feet and took his coffee mug to the sink to wash up. Above the sound of the water running he said, 'That's rubbing salt into it a bit, isn't it?'

Annie took a last look at the veal pie browning in the oven and closed the door. 'I would have liked Matt and Dolly to have the barn. I would really, lad.'

'Then why didn't you –'

'Jack did come up with the idea first. At least it seemed so. And he's so . . . so . . .'

Self-willed, thought Henry. But he didn't utter the words. 'You were afraid he'd throw up everything and go off elsewhere if we blocked his idea of having the barn?' he suggested.

'It's always at the back of my mind, Henry. Ever since you told me you financed the organic farming at Hathersage's just to prevent that very thing.'

'D'you really think it's a possibility?'

'Well, he's got to fend for his own, hasn't he? And just as Matt has Dolly to think on, Jack's got Pat.'

'But Annie . . . !' He was going to say, Pat would have the whole of Emmerdale Farmhouse if they gave up the barn to Matt. Yet he suddenly saw that it wasn't so. What Pat would have was a house shared with her mother-in-law. And though Annie was the easiest woman in the world to live with there must be a difference in attitudes, ways of doing things, customs, methods.

'Bit of a fix, isn't it?' he muttered. 'I know for a fact there's nowt here that we could buy for 'em, because I've enquired.'

'We couldn't afford it if there were.' As Henry opened his mouth to speak she added: 'And they wouldn't let you buy it for them, Henry, so you can forget about that.'

'They need never have known, Annie! That's what I'm kicking myself about! I could have foreseen all this months ago and got something going on the quiet. But no, I never even thought of it.'

'Don't blame yourself, Henry. We're all as bad as each other.'

'Except Joe,' Henry said. 'Joe's been trying to warn us ever since we voted that barn to Jack.'

Annie's father had come in as they spoke of blame. He was taking off his earthy boots on the door mat. He pushed his feet into slippers and came forward, offering a large cos lettuce and a bunch of shallots in a small basket. But his eyes were on them in a way that showed he had heard their words.

'Dad ought to be told, I think,' Annie said.

'Told what? What are you blaming each other for?'

Annie took the garden produce to the sink, ran water into a bowl to clean the lettuce. Trying to make it sound undramatic she said, 'Matt's been offered a job at N.Y. Estates and he's thinking of taking it.'

Sam sought his familiar chair. He sat down with a sigh of relief for his aching back. 'Well, don't say I didn't warn you,' he remarked.

Annie turned to regard him with surprise. 'Did you warn us?'

'I told you I thought Matt and Dolly should have had that barn.'

'Aye, it's the fact that N.Y. can offer a house that's the bugbear,' acknowledged Henry.

The old man leaned back in comfort then made ready to say something. They could tell it was important from the frown he directed first at his daughter, then Henry. 'I'll tell you summat you perhaps haven't considered. We lost Joe to N.Y. Estates, and managed. We could lose Jack, and manage. But one thing'll ditch Emmerdale good and proper, and that's losing Matt Skilbeck. He's the backbone of this farm, and if you don't know that by now you're closing your eyes to truth. *And*,' he ended, wagging a forefinger, 'Dolly knows it if you don't.'

His daughter nodded. 'We know that, Dad. We're not fools.'

'Then why don't the pair of you act as if you know it? I understand Dolly's feelings perfectly. She's fed up of seeing Matt treated as if he weren't important. She'd like a bit more appreciation.'

'We have always appreciated Matt, Dad!' Annie said with vehemence. 'How can you speak as if we haven't? He's been part of this family, like Joe and Jack.'

'How is it he wasn't treated like Jack over the barn, then?'

Henry drew a deep breath. 'Jack asked first.'

'And he's the eldest son,' Annie ended for him.

'Eldest son's place is here!' Sam cried. He pointed his finger at the floor of the kitchen. 'Here on the same ground his forebears lived. In the same house, doing the same job. Flighty-tighting about adapting a barn – that's not for the man who's going to inherit!'

'But Jack has a right –'

'Jack has a duty! Let's hear a bit less about Jack's rights. Let's hear more about his duty.'

'His first duty is to his wife and family, Sam,' Henry put in mildly, seeing the old man getting too intense. 'He has to think of Pat and the children.'

'The children will be grown soon and leaving the nest. Oh, it'll be a great situation in a year or two, won't it? Jackie gone off, Sandie at college or married, Pat and Jack in the barn, and you and me, Annie, left to rattle about here like a couple o' dried peas on a drum! Is that sense? I can't see that it is!'

Annie had given up her chore. She was turned about now, leaning against the sink, hands wrapped in the folds of her apron. The picture her father painted was not very attractive. And, as he said, it lacked sense. Her own instinct told her that the eldest son should live in the house of his fathers.

Yet Jack had already made his preference known. He wanted to live in the barn.

'Jack's shown what he wants. It was his own idea about the barn.'

'I'd like to hear what his idea will be when he discovers he'll be expected to run Emmerdale on his own after Matt's gone,' Sam said with a snort of derision. 'Jack may have some daft ideas but he's not entirely a fool. He knows he can't run Emmerdale.' He glared at the others. 'I suppose you do understand that he mustn't be let try?'

'Aye,' Henry said with a sigh. 'I'm afraid you're right. Sorry, Annie, but it's true.'

'I know it, Henry. He's my son but I know he's not a good farmer.' Not yet, she added inwardly. She always hoped her son was learning as he worked at Emmerdale.

'You reckon we should persuade Jack to give up the barn to Matt, Sam?' Henry asked. He was putting into words the thought that had been in his own mind yet too awkward to utter.

'Persuade him? If he's sense enough to see what losing Matt would mean, he won't need persuading.'

'I think you're forgetting Pat,' Annie intervened.

'That's Jack's problem, lass.'

But Annie knew more of the strains of sharing a home than her father. She could imagine how Pat would feel at losing the chance of a place of her own. With Dolly it had been different: there had been no problem because Dolly had been overwhelmingly happy at marrying Matt – so much so that simply to be with him had been enough. And then Dolly had never had a home over which she had been housewife. She had fitted into the ways of Emmerdale without demur.

With Pat it was different, and Annie knew it. There were the two children to see to – not without some strains and problems. It was difficult to deal with such things in front of an audience. There was the fact that Pat was a mature woman with her own preferences, her own view of how to run things. Annie knew that in Pat's place, she would be longing for a house to call her own.

If she were in Pat's place, perhaps she wouldn't give up the barn without a struggle...

'What we ought to do,' Henry was saying, 'is ring Joe and get him here. We need to know what Joe thinks.'

'Joe'll agree with me,' Sam said. 'In some things that lad's got sense.'

'Aye, Dad, but we ought to have him here. In a way, what we're doing is holding an emergency meeting of Emmerdale Farm Limited.'

'We can't do that, Annie. Not without informing Jack. And we need to discuss this without Jack being present.'

'Ring Joe,' urged Sam. 'Get him here and talk it through, no matter what you call the meeting. I guarantee he'll agree you should reverse that daft decision to award the barn to Jack.'

Henry nodded and, after a glance at Annie for permission, picked up the phone. Annie busied herself with the salad for the midday meal. The time for it was fast approaching, and though Jack had said he'd take a snack with Pat at the Woolpack, she expected Matt and Dolly indoors by about one. She was taking the pie out of the oven to cool when Henry replaced the receiver. 'Joe'll be here in about ten minutes.'

'He knows what it's about?'

'He guessed, I think. He sounded mighty relieved when I said it was a sort of summit conference.'

Sam Pearson got to his feet. 'I'll make myself scarce,' he remarked.

'Nay, Sam –'

'It's best. You're going to have a sort o' board meeting, and I'm not a member of the board.'

'But your opinion on this is important.'

'I've given my opinion,' he said. 'You know what I think. As far as I can see, there's no argument about what has to be done. It's simply how to do it – and that's up to you, isn't it? *I* can't do owt because I've no authority.'

'Have we?' Henry wondered aloud. 'Can we rescind an agreement if Jack refuses to listen?'

Sam grinned with some wry amusement. 'That's another reason I don't want to be here,' he said. 'I might express myself a bit forcible, about one or two things Jack's done. And I don't want Joe to hear me – Joe's got his own opinion of Jack and I don't want to seem to take sides with him.'

'But it is a family matter, Sam,' Henry insisted. 'It's more a family matter than a business matter. You have a right to state your opinion.'

'It's because it's a family matter that it's best left in your hands, Henry. You're able to stand back a bit. So I'm off upstairs to wash and change – I've an appointment in Beckindale this afternoon wi' the Horticultural Committee so I want to get tidied up any road.'

With that he trudged out. Henry looked at Annie. 'He feels all this a lot more keenly than he shows,' she said with a sigh. 'He's . . . disappointed in Jack.'

'I thought he'd got over all that about the divorce and the marriage and so on?'

'He's come to terms with it, because t'vicar told him it was his duty as a Christian. But he's not got over it, and this business about Matt and Dolly and the barn only reinforces his view that Jack doesn't look deeply into anything, just follows his own wishes.'

'That's not so, Annie. Jack has principles, just as his Grandad has.'

She smiled at him for defending her own son to her. 'I know that, lad. I just wish they were more easy to understand.'

A moment later they heard the N.Y. Land-Rover draw up outside. Annie went to the door to throw it open for Joe. 'Thanks for coming so quick, Joe.'

'Should you be somewhere else?' Henry asked as Joe came inside.

'I should be looking for Teddy Hooson, who's gone missing from his work.'

'Not again?'

'Aye, and hanged if I know what's to do. But I'm regarding this as me dinnertime. Well, what have you decided?'

'Decided? Joe, have a heart! We're only just beginning to understand the implications of Matt's job prospects!'

Joe sat down at the kitchen table, as if it were a board meeting. Annie, after a momentary glance at the vegetables she ought to be preparing, did likewise.

'The way I see it is this,' Joe said. 'You know now that Matt's been offered a damned good job with N.Y. Estates. He's also been offered a damned good house, which will be modernized to a standard Emmerdale could never match. On t'face of it, it's "an offer he can't refuse", as the saying goes.'

'And Dolly wants him to take it,' Henry said.

'Did he tell you that?'

'More or less. And your Grandad has said something

136

very important –'

'Grandad? Is he in on this?'

'He sees a lot more than you ever give him credit for, Joe,' his mother rebuked. 'And he said Dolly takes it to heart that Matt isn't taken account of enough here at Emmerdale.'

'What does that mean?' Joe enquired in surprise. 'Matt's equal partner here – he always was, even before he inherited Peggy's share. Him and me, we worked together and made the place what it is today. Everybody knows that.'

There was an uncomfortable silence. Then Henry said: 'Happen things have changed a bit since you left. You know Jack tends to go off at half-cock. I gather there have been quite a few occasions when he hasn't taken Matt into his confidence.'

'Oh aye. You mean, like when he bought those so-called bargain calves, that died in two days.' Joe nodded. 'There've been other things like that?'

'He never mentioned them to you?'

'Oh, you know Matt. He'd never say a harsh word about anybody, let alone us at Emmerdale.'

'Well, of course he tells Dolly. Or at least, she senses things.' Henry shook his head in regret. 'The long and the short of it is, Dolly has other reasons besides the house for wanting Matt to take the job with N.Y.'

'And Matt goes along with her?'

'Nay, Matt's very unwilling to leave. And so's Dolly, really. It's just that . . .'

'It's just that, now she sees what Turner would offer, she realizes he's getting short-changed here at Emmerdale?'

Joe, having said this, regretted it; for his mother made a little exclamation of distress.

'I'm sorry, Ma. I don't mean that as harshly as it sounded. But you have to look at the facts. Matt is a fully qualified shepherd. He wins awards at county shows. He makes a good profit by the sale of his sheep, and the wool's good. He contributes a large slice of the Emmerdale profits.'

'I'll vouch for that,' Henry said, thinking of the entries in the accounts that were to the credit of Matt.

'Then besides all that, Matt's a good cowman – his heart's not in it to the same extent as the shepherding, but he knows what he's doing and he's never been found wanting there. He can do drainage, he can drive almost any kind of machine that's in use in the district, he's handy with tools, and he's . . . he's honest and hardworking and an ideal employee. So why on earth shouldn't he be wanted by Alan Turner at a wage that he deserves and with a nice snug house to go with it?'

Annie had been giving a little shake of her head at this recital. 'Put like that,' she said, 'have we the right to try to keep him?'

'Oh yes,' said Henry. 'He gave me that right when he came to me to ask for a solution to the problem. It's not a matter of money with Matt. It's a matter of . . . well, of being where he belongs. And he feels he belongs at Emmerdale. But not if his wife has to suffer.'

'It's true Dolly hasn't been herself for quite a while now,' Annie admitted. 'ever since that meeting about the barn . . .'

'I couldn't come out in the open and say Turner was fishing for Matt,' Joe said. 'I had to keep it confidential. I'm sorry, Ma – it was a business secret.'

'Yes, I understand. But to tell the truth, we shouldn't have needed to be told we were being neglectful. We should have realized it ourselves.'

'But now you know, what are you going to do?'

'Your Grandad says we should ask Jack to give up the barn to Matt.'

Joe shrugged about on his chair. 'Some hopes,' he muttered. 'It's the obvious solution, but will he do it?'

'It's either that, or Matt leaves. And then what do we do? Even Jack must see we couldn't run the farm without Matt,' Henry said.

Annie tried not to show how it hurt her to hear those words, 'Even Jack.' 'I think he'll understand once the facts –'

'He might try hiring somebody,' Joe said. 'Plenty of good men looking for a job these days.'

'Nobody as good as Matt.'

'No, but Jack's got to understand that point. There isn't

a man you could hire between here and John o' Groats that would work as hard or as uncomplainingly as Matt. You could get another pair of hands – but you couldn't get the willingness.'

'Besides,' Henry said, 'a point we've all forgotten – Matt is a shareholder in the farm. If he leaves, would he want to sell his share?'

'He wouldn't!' Annie exclaimed.

'Well, he might, Ma. He could make a big profit – a lot of folk are looking for a chance to buy into farming these days.'

'But he wouldn't,' she insisted.

'I think you're right, but it would make sense. And if someone like Alan Turner began giving him advice, he might see it was to his advantage to sell out and put his money into N.Y. Estates instead.'

'Is that what you really think, Henry?'

'No, but we ought to consider it. We've all been so damned thoughtless over this.'

'Except Joe,' said Annie, with a grateful glance towards her younger son.

'And my hands were tied,' he said. 'I can tell you, it's been no fun these last few days, watching Alan getting his hooks into Matt.'

Henry cleared his throat and rapped on the table with his knuckles. 'Sitha,' he said, 'we've scared ourselves enough with the possibilities of doom if Matt leaves. We're all united in thinking Matt must be prevented from leaving. Right?'

'Right,' Joe said with vehemence, while Annie looked agreement.

'Matt doesn't want to leave, so we don't have to make an equivalent offer to N.Y. All we have to do is offer Matt and Dolly a suitable home.'

'And that's the old barn for conversion,' said Joe.

'So we're agreed, aren't we, that we have to ask Jack to give it up and let Matt have it?'

'Agreed,' said Joe.

'Agreed,' said Annie.

'Right you are. Who's going to put it to him?'

There was a pause. 'Well, I can't,' said Joe. 'In the first

place, he'd only think I was getting in a dig at him –'

'Joe!'

'It's true, Ma, you know it is. And in the second place, I don't think it would come well from an employee of N.Y. Estates to try and frustrate the plans of the estate manager. I mean, I'll do it if you think I'm the best person, but I think I'm the worst.'

'What about you, Annie? Would you take it on?'

She stared down at the table. 'I will if you ask me to. But I don't want to. It will mean, if Jack agrees, that he'll have to remain here in the house. And I don't ever want him to think – or Pat either – that I'm a possessive mother who wouldn't let him live a few yards away.'

'He wouldn't think that, Annie!' But he could see she was fundamentally unwilling to seem interfering in her son's married life. 'All right,' he grunted, 'it seems I'm elected. I'll ask him to come to the Woolpack this afternoon and put it to him. Is that agreed?'

Annie and Joe said yes, and that was the end of the discussion, or so they thought. But they were wrong.

They heard the sound of the farm's Land-Rover drawing up outside, and then Jack himself came hurrying in. He drew up short when he saw his younger brother.

'I've been looking all over N.Y. land for you!' he exclaimed.

'Have you? What for?' Joe said in surprise, then paused as he remembered his glimpse of young Jackie Merrick with his face all cut and bruised, disappearing over the fields. Had it something to do with that?

'I'll tell you what for!' Jack stormed. 'I want an explanation, for of all the dirty tricks a man can play on his own family, this takes some beating!'

'Jack, I won't have this kind of thing in my house,' his mother reproved. 'You've no cause to –'

'Oh yes I have! I've good cause! Joe and his mates at N.Y. Estates are out to poach Matt off us!'

Chapter Eleven

It was only to be expected that Joe would react angrily to the accusation. 'Now you just hold on a minute!'

'Don't say you didn't know! Alan Turner wants Matt as a replacement for Jesse Gillan when he retires.'

'We know that, lad,' his mother said in a tone of rebuke.

Jack was stopped short. 'You what? Did – did he tell you that?'

'No I didn't!' Joe said in annoyance. 'And I'd like to know what you mean by coming in here chucking accusations about like birdseed! You've no royal rights over Matt, and nor has anyone else! If he gets a good offer from N.Y., he'll make up his mind about it without our interference.'

'But not without N.Y.'s bribery! Or your connivance!'

'Oh, for God's sake! Can't you ever see anyone else's side but your own?'

Annie startled them all by banging the table with her fist. 'Shut up the pair of you!' she ordered.

'But he came roaring in here –'

'The point is, Ma –'

'I said shut up! And sit down!'

Her two sons, who had been on their feet shouting at each other, subsided in sullen silence on the nearest chairs. Annie then said: 'We'll talk about this quietly and sensibly, or not at all.' She gave them a hard glance and when they didn't disagree she said to Henry, 'I apologize for my sons, Henry.'

'Ma, I've done nothing to apologize for –' Joe began.

'You've shouted in front of me in my kitchen. That's why I'm apologizing to Henry for you.' Annie turned to Jack. 'As for you! It seems to me you're too fond of shouting thief before the horse has even put its nose outside the stable door. Shouldn't a lad of your intelligence know better than to make accusations without knowing the facts?'

Jack gave her a bitter stare. 'If it comes to knowing facts – how long have you known Joe was trying to filch Matt for

N.Y. Estates?'

'Only since yesterday. But I don't agree with your view of it.'

'I'll bet *he* didn't tell you!'

'Matt told Henry,' she said.

'Told Henry? Yesterday?' Henry nodded. Jack resumed: 'And how long have *you* known?'

Joe had a hard struggle not to erupt into anger again. But respect for his mother restrained him. 'What difference does it make how long I've known?'

'I'd have thought it makes a lot of difference. Because it shows where your loyalties lie.'

Henry had held his peace in face of the storm that was raging. He knew it was time to speak up now. 'Now wait a minute, Jack. If it comes to loyalties, does it slip your mind that Joe couldn't come racing to us with the news because that would have been betraying a confidence?'

'Well, I–'

'There's ethics in business, lad, just as everywhere else. And I think you ought to stop and think about that. And while you're thinking, I'll just lay a few more things on the line.' He glanced at Annie. 'I'm the only one here that's not a Sugden, so happen it's best I speak up.'

She gave a frowning gesture. 'I don't see what that has to do –'

'I do, Annie. Remember what Sam said about not wanting it to be a family matter.' He glanced at the two men with some authority. 'I'm speaking now as chairman of Emmerdale Farm Limited and calling an Extraordinary General Meeting. There are enough of us here to form a quorum. All in favour say "Aye".' He waited. 'Come on,' he said, 'speak up. If you say "Nay" I'm resigning on the spot, for I'll not stay chairman of a company that's nowt but a squabbling family.'

There was no refusing that tone. 'Aye' said everyone, somewhat sheepishly, although a faint twinkle had dawned in Annie's eye.

'Now let's face this as people of business,' he went on, tapping the table with a forefinger. 'If anyone – N.Y. or anyone else – wants to offer Matt a good job, they've every right to do so, and there's nowt anybody can do to stop 'em.

142

It so happens that Joe has a foot in both camps, Emmerdale and N.Y. Knowing this Alan Turner – quite properly in my view – explicitly forbade Joe to play any part in the affair and made the offer to Matt himself.'

'But Joe knew.'

'Of course he knew. But he had been told the approach was confidential and he was not to mention it to any of us at Emmerdale.'

Jack said something in a muffled tone which seemed to imply that he wasn't persuaded by any of that.

'I'll tell you, since you need to have it spelled out,' Henry said with some impatience, 'that Joe did drop various hints about looking after Matt, but that's as far as he could go and live with his conscience. *Now*,' and he took a breath as if to show he was embarking on a different tack, 'the nub of the problem is this. Matt wants a cottage; we can't afford to buy him one; N.Y. Estates have got one ready and waiting.'

'Hah!' said Jack.

'What d'you mean, "hah"?' Henry demanded with some irritation. 'They've a right to offer what they've got. They've a right to try for the best man for the job. What d'you expect them to do – hire morons so they won't compete with us?'

'Well, I . . . I only meant . . . Of course they've got resources they can use . . .'

'You bet they've got resources! But for all that, Matt don't want to leave Emmerdale. He's told me that quite frankly. Yet he and Dolly want a house of their own. Dolly in particular feels it's due to Matt, considering his importance to us.'

'And your attitude when you came rushing in here proves how important you think he is,' Joe put in, with considerable calm.

'Alan Turner,' said Henry, 'has been cute enough to spot the difficulty over getting a house for them –'

'Because you told him, I suppose!' Jack exclaimed to Joe.

'I never meant to. I asked for Tolly's Farmhouse for them to rent. It never occurred to me that he'd use it as bait to catch Matt.'

Jack, hearing this, began to look a little less certain of himself. Henry viewed him with some severity and continued: 'The situation as of now is, if Matt don't get a cottage or house from us, he's going to N.Y. What are we going to do about it?'

There was a pause that seemed to go on for ever. Then Jack said to Joe: 'I apologize.'

Joe coloured up. 'Forget it,' he said. 'But think before you speak next time.'

After that, no one else spoke. The three who had conferred earlier knew that it all depended now on Jack. He said at length: 'We can't afford to lose Matt. We couldn't manage without him.'

Heads nodded agreement.

'I know what's going on in your minds,' he went on. 'Let him have the barn. Right?'

His mother gave a little shrug. 'No one here is going to say anything to influence you one way or the other, Jack.'

'But it's one of those times when silence speaks volumes, though, isn't it?'

'It was agreed you'd have the barn. No one's going to take it from you, lad.'

'But you want me to give it up.' He looked from one face to the other, and read the same message in each. 'I'll have to put it to Pat. It won't be easy.'

'Well, brother, try managing without Matt and see if that's easy,' Joe reminded him.

'I know, I know . . .' He was deep in thought. 'Matt and Dolly will be in in a minute. Don't mention this to them in case it doesn't work.'

It's got to work, thought Joe as he took his leave while his mother hastily got on with preparations for the meal. It's got to work or it's goodbye to anything like good management at Emmerdale.

Henry likewise left Emmerdale. He felt guilty about neglecting the Woolpack for so long, but he needn't have worried. He found Amos too immersed in journalism to upbraid him for his absence.

'Mr Wilks! Mr Wilks, I'm so glad you're back! Mr Wilks, I want you to take over at once. I've got to go out – I've a scoop on my hands!'

144

For a minute Henry had a mental vision of a scoop – a small handled shovel for measuring sugar or flour. Then he understood that his partner was speaking in reportorial capacity. 'Something big, is it?'

'The biggest thing in Beckindale for months! D'you know what I've been told, Mr Wilks? Half the crops on N.Y.'s land have been poisoned!'

'You what?'

'Poisoned, Mr Wilks! Made unfit for human consumption!'

'You sure, Amos?' Henry queried, watching with a tolerant eye as Amos stooped to put on his bicycle clips.

'I have it on the highest authority –'

'Only I've just been talking to Joe, and he never mentioned a word about it.'

'Well, he wouldn't, would he? You can be assured them at N.Y. wouldn't want it known. But I can tell you, Mr Wilks, summat dastardly's been done to the crops.'

'Really? Whereabouts?'

'That's just what I'm off to find out! I shall cycle round until I see the evidence, and then they won't be able to deny –'

'It'll be a fair cycle ride, Amos. N.Y. Estate's a long piece to cover on a bike.'

'That's where my instincts as a reporter come in, you see,' Amos said. He wheeled his bike out of the shed at the back where it was kept. Henry stood in the doorway to watch him take it out to the back gate. 'I'll be back afore evening opening, Mr Wilks.'

'I certainly hope so,' Henry said to himself as he saw him wobble off. He never had much faith in Amos's ability to stay upright on the bike.

The custom in the Woolpack was only light, as it generally was on a weekday at noon. As he was thinking of putting the cloth over the pumps, Matt Skilbeck came in with Dolly.

'Thought I'd bring Dolly out for a little treat,' he confided to Henry as he bought drinks. 'She's been in Hotten all morning trying to match some wool – got right tired out, and worse still she looked in some estate agents' windows and scared herself at the prices they're asking.'

145

'I'm sorry about that, Matt. Have these on me, then.'

'Nay, Henry –'

'Go on. It's little enough, goodness knows.'

'Henry,' Matt said as he turned with the drinks in his hands. 'Any ideas on . . . you know?'

'We-ell . . . I've had a long discussion wi' some of the folk concerned.'

'Did anything come of it?'

'It's too early to say, Matt.'

'I dunno if that's true, Henry. I'm expecting Alan Turner to come after me almost any minute now, and I must have *summat* to say to him.'

'Just hold him off for a bit, that's all I ask, Matt.'

'Righto. And Dolly? What am I to tell Dolly?'

'Tell her I'm doing everything I can think of to help solve the problem.'

Matt nodded and with a sigh took the drinks to Dolly at the table outside where she had settled to feel the warm sunshine.

'Has he anything to suggest, love?' she asked. 'About the job?'

'Not yet. He says he's working on it.'

'I wonder if even Henry can do owt?'

'Come on, now, lass, drink up and stop being so down. It's not good for you to get depressed.'

She managed a little laugh. 'You know expectant mums have funny moods. It's all to do with hormones.'

'So long as it's a mood I can improve with a vodka and orange, all right. Just don't start wanting champagne and caviar!'

In the meantime, Jack was going about the various tasks he had still to do at Emmerdale before it was time to bring in the cows for evening milking. He was up at the far end of the north pasture clearing weeds from the drinking channel when his mother appeared at the far edge. She waved to him to come. He straightened with a feeling of relief and came to her, his hands wet with the cool water but smarting from the stinging nettles.

'Jack, Mr Hinton was on the phone. He says will you ring him back, or better still, will you drop by and see him.'

146

'Anything urgent?'

'He said he'd like to speak to you today, if possible.'

Jack raised his thick dark brows. Something to do with that strange escapade of Jackie's, perhaps? 'Righto, Ma, I'll drop in on him afore I go to collect Pat from Home Farm after milking.'

There was constraint between him and Matt as they worked together in the milking parlour. Matt was thinking about Henry and whatever hopes he might supply. Jack was thinking, belatedly, that he had whisked away the old barn from under Matt's nose and never paused to understand how much it had upset him.

He wanted to say, 'Listen, Matt, I'm sorry for being so obtuse.' But it was better to wait until he'd spoken to Pat and had her permission to hand over the barn.

It did cross his mind to wonder if that would satisfy Dolly now. The house N.Y. were promising was a much better place – soundly built, ready to occupy as it stood and, with the improvements N.Y. would do, probably about to turn into a right little palace.

And the money, too . . . Jack knew how high the wages were at N.Y. Estates. Their workmen were given bonuses and good overtime, and special allowances for special training. At those rates, Matt could at least double his earnings, perhaps do even better.

Good Lord, Jack said to himself, we just never realized how lucky we were to have him. It's a true saying – you never miss the water until the well runs dry. And then he had honesty enough to add: Happen I was the only one who didn't value Matt at his just deserts. Joe's always thought highly of him, and Ma looks on him as the salt of the earth. Well, it's not too late to show him I think a lot of him too.

He tidied himself up briskly after milking and set off to see the vicar, with a fair amount of curiosity over what could be in the air. Mr Hinton welcomed him with some gravity.

'I must say,' he said, breaking into a faint smile, 'it's unusual to have you come to my home twice in one day, Jack.'

Jack suppressed a little gesture of annoyance. The vicar knew he wasn't a believer. What was the use of pointing it out?

'Is this about Jackie?' he asked.

'Yes, it is. I'm sure you have a lot of curiosity over the reason for that scene this morning.'

'I hoped to have it out with him this evening.'

'I sincerely hope you won't "have it out" with him, Jack. The boy doesn't deserve treatment that could be described in that way. He's done nothing wrong.'

'Oh no? Scrapping with someone and coming away from it looking like a tough?'

'He had a fight with Teddy Hooson.'

'Teddy Hooson?' Jack had to search his mind to remember who that was. 'Oh, that awful kid that Sandie's keen on. Ah,' he said, light dawning. 'He had a fight over Sandie?'

'No, he had a fight over you.'

'Me?'

'Yes, you. That surprises you?'

Jack got his breath back. 'It astonishes me. I never thought Jackie would raise a hand over anything to do with me.'

'Well, perhaps it would be more accurate to say that Jackie was standing up for the cause of truth. He caught Teddy out in a lie, and challenged him on it.'

To say that Jack was amazed was putting it mildly. 'Since when has Jackie been so concerned to uphold the cause of truth? I always got the impression he cared about almost nothing.'

'That's sad. Strange how two people who should be close can be so much at variance.'

I didn't come here for a sermon, thought Jack. But he had enough curiosity to want to know more. 'So what was this truth he was upholding?'

Mr Hinton turned away, so that the other man shouldn't see the faint crease of disapproval between his brows. Really, Jack Sugden was surprisingly slow to catch a nuance. He had hoped he would sense how important this was.

'As I understand it, Teddy has caused some disaster to happen to a large crop of potatoes, and arranged matters so that you should get the blame.'

'Me? But I never go on N.Y. land! How could it be me?'

'You returned some chemicals recently, I believe.'

'Yes, di-methoate.'

'That was the name. Teddy emptied the contents of a canister away and refilled it with weedkiller. He then put that into the spray-tank for his tractor – and another canister too, I seem to recall – and deliberately sprayed it on the potatoes. His aim was to have it thought that you had got into the storehouse and switched the harmless spray for the weedkiller.'

'Good God!' Jack sat down on the sofa. He went first hot then cold with anger. 'That young devil! What did I ever do to him? Well, I'll have him in court –'

'I think not, Jack. From what I've been able to learn this afternoon, N.Y. Estates are hushing the matter up.'

'But that . . . that's almost obscene! A lad can plan a thing like this, ruin a crop, arrange for someone else to get the blame, and nothing is done? By the Lord, I'll see to it that –'

'Perhaps the Lord has already taken a hand. Jackie has done His work for Him, to some extent. A few punches landed where they would hurt most . . . Yes, He did once turn the money-changers out of the temple with scant ceremony. He wouldn't disapprove, perhaps.'

'So Jackie thumped him! Good for him ! But it does seem a bit thick that N.Y. are going to let it go at that.'

'Well, perhaps something more will happen. Teddy's career may suffer a check from now on. Once the story gets to them, I imagine they won't be giving him much responsibility.'

'But how are they going to hear of it? It's no use me going to them – they don't listen to anything I have to say.'

The vicar was moving about the room with his hands clasped behind his back. 'Mr Turner is a churchgoer. I don't think, frankly, that he attends out of any desire to praise his Maker, it's more to play his part in the community. But it does allow me the chance to drop a hint.'

'And you'll do that? Because, honestly, vicar – that boy's not safe to have around! If there was evidence that would stand up in court, that's where he belongs.'

'It's a matter of Jackie's word against his, I believe. It would get nowhere in court, even if Mr Turner would prosecute. Which he won't.'

'That's big business for you!' Jack snorted. 'Well, thanks, Mr Hinton, for telling me about this. I'll talk it over with Jackie.'

'By no means!' Hinton cried, whirling. 'You've misunderstood the situation. The last thing Jackie wants is to have to talk to you. His words to me were: "When he talks to me it's only to criticize and when I talk to him it's only to put myself further in the wrong."'

'But that's terrible!' Jack was aghast. 'He's done this good thing –'

'He did more, Jack. I haven't finished explaining. Jackie didn't hit Teddy just because he caught him out in a lie. He hit him because Teddy made some improper remarks about yourself and his mother. In a word, he was championing you.'

For a long moment Jack said nothing. He went slowly red under his outdoor tan. Then he said, 'I *must* speak to him. I must say thank you, at least.'

'He doesn't want your thanks. If you were to offer them, he'd say he did it for his mother and not for you. I do seriously advise you to leave things alone for the present. Now is not the time.'

'Then when? Vicar, he's my son!'

'All the more reason to be careful. You know that Freud said the family was the great battle-ground. Much though I disapprove of some of his sayings, that one strikes me as true.'

A battle-ground. Yes, it was impossible to disagree. And at present, Jack didn't feel like a victor.

He drove on to collect Pat from Home Farm. She wasn't waiting at Verney Lane end as she usually was. He got out and walked up the lane to the posts of the drive, which still carried the old heraldic beasts of the Verney family. It was a warm, glowing July evening, the air full of the scent of stock from the flowerbeds that Turner maintained as part of the good appearance of the place. Big old chestnut trees cast a pleasant shade. Hoverflies buzzed among the rhododendrons.

When Pat showed up at last she was walking slowly, almost reluctantly. If Jack hadn't been so preoccupied he might have noticed she had red-rimmed eyes.

'Hullo, love, you're a bit late?'

'Not very.'

They fell into step together. He opened the passenger door of the Land-Rover, his mind still busy on other things. After they drove off they spoke very little. Once over the bridge and into Beckindale High Street, Jack avoided the turning to Emmerdale but instead took the Connelton road. Pat didn't even remark on it. He turned the vehicle into a farm track and parked, choosing a spot under a big old thorn tree.

'I've something serious to ask you, Pat,' he said.

She looked at him. She was pale, and if he had been examining her expression he'd have seen apprehension as well as distress.

But Jack was gazing out through the windscreen at the landscape. It answered some deep need within him. He wanted peace – peace above everything. The family is the great battle-ground . . . How was it that a man could mean well, and yet cause so much ill-will and unhappiness?

'I seem to have a talent for it,' he muttered.

'What?'

'Nothing. Let's get out and breathe the air.'

They made their way to the old stone wall, moss-speckled. It was warm to the touch. Jack leaned his back against it. 'Are you all that set on having the old barn converted?' he asked.

It seemed to take Pat by surprise. She said on an outblown breath: 'What?'

'It seems someone else has a better claim, Pat.'

'What are you talking about?'

'About Matt – Matt and Dolly. Dolly desperately wants a home of her own, for the baby, you know . . . And Matt's been offered this marvellous job with N.Y. Estates.' He explained the situation to her. It didn't dawn on him that she was only half-listening.

Her real attention was elsewhere, on the words her son had spoken to her before she left Home Farm. He had sought her out in the little cubby-hole, formerly the butler's pantry, where she hung her coat and kept the few possessions she'd brought to the office.

151

'I've made up my mind, Mum,' he began.

'Oh? About what?'

'I've decided I don't want to live at Emmerdale.'

'Jackie!' She had been putting on lipstick in front of a little pocket mirror propped on the window sill. She turned at the words. 'What d'you mean?'

'I've decided to move out.'

'But you can't! What on earth are you saying? You can't move out!'

'I can, Mum, and I'm doing it. I'll fetch my gear some time –'

'Jackie! Jackie, I don't understand!' She was totally bewildered. Everything had been going so well at Emmerdale: Mrs Sugden so kind to them all, the old grandfather taken with the children and particularly Jackie, and the children settling in with satisfaction to a routine of plentiful meals, regular hours . . .

'There's nowt for you to understand. I've just decided not to live at Emmerdale. I'm old enough to make up my own mind where I live, you know.' He was speaking roughly, to hide the fact that he was as emotional about it as she was.

'But where would you go, Jackie! You can't just –'

'I'll go back to the van, Mum. Lucky I've left a lot of my stuff there anyhow.'

'You can't live there!'

'I did afore. Why can't I now?'

'But on your own, Jackie? You can't!'

'Yes I can. I'm old enough!'

'That's not the point! Who'd look after you – cook your meals, do your wash?'

'I can cook for myself.'

'Oh yes!' Unexpectedly a laugh bubbled up – a laugh that was half a sob. 'You that's never lifted a hand for yourself all your life! You wouldn't know how to boil an egg!'

'I'll learn,' he said. 'And any road, there's tins and frozen –'

'Jackie, I won't have this!' She had had time to collect herself now. She tried to exert authority. 'I won't allow you to do a daft thing like this.'

But it was too late to try to exercise control over her son.

She had never done it before and she had chosen the wrong moment.

'I'm not arguing about it, Mum. I'm just telling you.' He came to her and patted her on the shoulder, awkwardly, as if she were a pet dog. 'I've thought it through and I've come to the conclusion it's best for everybody.'

'What rubbish! Best for everybody? It's not best for you, and it's certainly not best for *me*!'

'It is, Mum. It really is.' The young voice trembled with earnestness. 'I thought it might work the other way, but it's not going to.'

'What is it? What's happened?'

'Nowt. It's nothing for you to worry about.'

'Jackie, what happened to your face?' In the poor light of the little room she'd just been able to distinguish the sticking plaster on his forehead and the darker skin of the bruising.

'I got in a fight – it's nothing.'

'Who? Who did you fight?'

'Oh, never mind –'

'Tell me, Jackie!' All kinds of nightmare ideas rushed into her head. Had he had a fight with Jack? There was always animosity seething below the surface of Jackie's attitude to her husband. 'I've got to know!' she cried, seizing his hand. 'Who did you fight?'

'Oh, it was only Teddy Hooson –'

'Teddy?' Like everyone else, her thoughts flew to Sandie. 'What has he done? Is it Sandie?'

'It's nowt to do with Sandie – though she's stupid to have anything to do with him, Mum; you ought to choke that off. He's a wrong 'un, after all.'

'What was it? What did he do?'

'Nothing for you to worry about. It's to do with N.Y. Estates. Him and me had a sparring match –'

'Oh, love,' she said, touching the plaster with a gentle finger. 'And you got the worst of it . . .'

'Not a bit. I gave him a right old busted jaw. Serve him right, the lying git. Lucky for him he's only going to be around another week or so – he's better off in Spalding wi' all his highly-trained cronies. I bet they all fiddle their time-sheets and steal diesel from the tanks . . .'

'I never liked him,' she agreed. 'But it's a pity you actually came to blows. Is that owt to do with wanting to live in the van?'

'In a way, in a way . . .' He shook his head. 'Don't ask me to explain it all now. I just feel I want to get away from . . . from . . .'

'From us?'

He sighed deeply. He could see she was never going to be satisfied with surface reasons. 'Listen, Mum,' he said, 'I want you to be happy – right? And as long as I'm around for Jack to stumble over, things are never going to run smooth atween you two. I'm always going to cause arguments –'

'What's happened now?' she cried in despair. 'Jack hasn't mentioned anything.'

'Nay, and happen that's best. If he'd just let things lay . . . But he always wants to discuss, and question, and criticize . . . And I can't stand it any more. I'm fed up of it. So I'm going to live in the caravan and get some peace.'

'That's not the solution, Jackie.'

'Happen. But at least it gives us some breathing space.' He sounded unexpectedly adult as he said it. He was quoting Mr Hinton who had recommended just that, although without expecting Jackie to remove bodily from Emmerdale.

'You're not going to live in that pokey little –'

'It's not so pokey – not for one. And it's got everything you need, hasn't it? And I'm an employee of N.Y. so I'm entitled to living accommodation.'

'They won't let you have it!' she cried, seizing on that. 'They won't think you're a suitable tenant.'

'Yes they will. I asked Joe and he said yes.'

'He said yes!'

He didn't report what Joe had said. When Jackie told him outright his reason for wanting the caravan – that he needed to get away from Jack – Joe had said with some sympathy, 'I know what you mean. Okay then, if your Mum don't object, go ahead. I'll have to ask Alan when he gets back but he won't bother one way or the other. In fact, it's better to have it occupied – keeps the vandals off.'

'So you see it's all fixed up, Mum. I'm going to the village shop now to get a few things –'

'Oh, Jackie, don't! Don't leave us like this!'

'I'm not going far.' Only far enough not to have to account for his actions to Jack Sugden.

'But what about Mrs Sugden? What's she going to say when I tell her?'

Jackie hadn't even thought of that. He was a little dismayed at the thought of hurting Annie's feelings, for she had been good to him.

'You can say it's convenient for getting out to the traps first thing in the morning –'

'She won't believe that!'

'Well then . . . tell her what you like.'

'It seems so ungrateful, after she took us in.'

'I'm sorry. I'll see her myself, then . . . I'll try to explain. I don't want her thinking badly of me.'

She could see he was totally determined. She gave in. 'All right.'

To her surprise he dropped a kiss on the top of her head. 'It's all right, I'm not going to Siberia, tha knows. Just across the fields, that's all. See you later.' And with that he went out to do his household shopping at the village store.

It was this scene which had depressed her so much before she went to meet her husband.

'So would you be prepared to give it up?' he was now asking.

'What? Give what up?'

'Pat, haven't you been listening? I'm talking about the barn! You can see that Emmerdale can't function without Matt.' Jack sighed and shrugged. 'There's nothing like being made to see things in their true perspective for cutting a man down to size. The minute I heard we might lose Matt, I knew the farm would grind to a halt without him. It stared me in the face – *I* couldn't run it. I've been kidding myself all this while.'

'Nay, love,' she said, roused to pity by the sadness in his tone. 'You're a hardworking farmer, eager to make a good job of it –'

'I'm a great clumsy idiot who puts his big feet in where he ought to walk on eggshells, Pat. I nearly lost Matt because I couldn't see what was plain as a pikestaff to

155

everybody else. And I still haven't got him unless you agree to give up the barn.'

'Oh, the barn!' she cried impatiently. 'I don't care about the barn!'

'You don't? But I thought . . .'

She quelled her impatience. He couldn't know that the chief part of her mind was busy with something else – the feeling that her son was slipping away from her. She said in a more moderate tone: 'I don't mind living in the farm really, Jack. Let Matt and Dolly have the barn. It don't matter that much to me, honestly.'

'You sure?'

'Perfectly.'

He put an arm about her and gave her a little quick hug. 'Thanks, love. That helps. But . . .'

'But what? What's the matter?'

He was hesitating. 'I got the wrong side of Jackie again –'

'You?'

'Yes, I jumped to conclusions and found out too late I'd misjudged him.'

'Over leaving Emmerdale – was that it?'

He stood upright and stared at her. 'Leaving Emmerdale? How d'you mean?'

'He just told me: he's moving out to the caravan.'

'He what? He can't do that! That's N.Y. property.'

'It's all right, he got Joe's permission.'

'He asked Joe? Without asking us first?'

'What does it matter whose permission he got, Jack? The awful fact is, he wants to go. He says he needs breathing space.'

Jack waited a moment, taking this in. 'He's talked to you about it?'

'Only to say he wants to move out. I can't seem to get any sense out of him. He wouldn't explain why.'

'I can tell you why,' Jack said with contrition, his dark eyes shadowed by the recollection. 'He had a fight with Teddy Hooson, and I happened to see him and tore him off a strip. Vicar's just explained to me – Hooson sprayed a field with Paraquat –'

'That hasn't happened,' Pat said quickly. 'N.Y. want no

156

publicity about it. They're just going to plough in the potatoes tomorrow and that's the end of it.'

'Well, it seems Teddy Hooson did it to get back at me. I can only suppose it's because I tried to stop him keeping Sandie out late. And perhaps it had something to do with revenge on Joe for sacking him. Jackie got in a fight with him – defending me, partly.' Jack shook his head. 'Nay, I think it were more to defend you – Hooson said summat that Jackie wouldn't take.'

'Oh, poor lad . . .' She recalled Jackie giving her his decision to leave. He had been so weary and determined.

'I suppose moving out to the caravan is my punishment for misjudging him,' Jack sighed.

She missed the fact that her husband viewed it from the point of view of his own part in it. She said with affection: 'Never mind. As he says himself, it's not Siberia. And it'll make things easier in the house, won't it?'

'D'you think so? Ma isn't going to think it's easier, losing her grandson. It's a shame . . . Ma's done nowt wrong, but she's a loser as much as any of us.'

She wanted to say, That's the way it is, don't you understand that? Pat had been a loser so often that she had become reconciled to it. She accepted defeat more readily than Jack, who still believed that you could manage life so that everything went well. If things went wrong, he felt, then someone was to blame – and on this occasion, it seemed to be himself.

'Taken all in all,' he remarked, 'I can't say I've covered myself with glory, the way I've handled things.'

'It's no use moaning about it, love. What's done is done.'

'Moaning?' He was quite hurt.

'Well, what else are you doing? And if you think about it, we've a lot to be thankful for. Matt will stay on and that's the most important thing.'

'Aye . . . Come on, we'd best get home to tea. Ma'll be wondering where we've got to.'

He couldn't help feeling some reluctance at having to break the news to her about Jackie. He felt he'd have to tell her everything on the basis of 'first the bad news' – first that Jackie was leaving and then that Matt was staying.

Swings and roundabouts . . . The good and the bad were

supposed to even themselves out. But he couldn't come to terms with the idea that he'd antagonized his own son to the extent that the boy couldn't share the same roof with him.

Everyone else was waiting to sit down to the meal when they got in. Dolly was puzzling over her knitting pattern while Matt sat alongside her on the sofa reading the newspaper. Annie at once began cutting the cold veal pie while Grandad held out his plate.

'Come on, hurry up, we're all starving,' he said.

'Jackie's not here yet, Grandad,' Sandie pointed out.

'Isn't he with you?' asked Annie, for sometimes Jack gave the boy a lift home with his mother.

'Nay, he won't be in. He's . . . er . . . he's decided to take over the caravan.'

Dolly looked up from her knitting. 'Take over? How d'you mean?'

'He's going to live there.' Jack looked around and added, 'For the present.'

'Nay, has all this talk about living accommodation given the lad the idea there's not room enough . . .'

'It's not that, Ma. He's had a long talk with the vicar. He's decided he wants to be on his own for a bit.'

Mention of the vicar stifled rejection of the idea. Annie looked down at the food she was serving. If she was disappointed she didn't show it. After a moment she said, 'How's he going to manage about his meals?'

'That remains to be seen.'

'I'd best put a piece of pie in a plastic bag and take it over after we've eaten,' she said, hiding her sorrow in practical decisions. 'A growing boy – he needs good food.'

'Well, there's something even more important to be said,' Jack remarked. 'Matt, I learned today from Henry that you talked to him about a possible job at N.Y. Estates.'

'Aye,' Matt said, coming slowly to the table and taking his place. Dolly had stood up, putting away her knitting in its bag. She was watching Jack closely.

'Well, you know we can't offer you the same kind of conditions you'd get there, Matt. But the chief problem seems to be housing. So I'd like to offer you the barn for conversion to a house to suit yourself and Dolly, and hope that'll make the offer from Alan Turner seem less attractive.'

'Oh, you lovely man!' cried Dolly, and swooped on him to give him a hug. 'Oh, Jack! It's what we really wanted.'

'But I thought you and Pat –'

'Nay, Matt, it's not important to me,' Pat said. 'I'm happy here in the farmhouse. I only wanted the barn as a way of spreading us out more – but that happens if it's you and Dolly in the barn and us here in the farmhouse.'

Sandie, listening and saying nothing, was thinking that no one had asked her opinion. She liked the farmhouse, she was pleased with her little room, but it would have been nice to have a new little house made specially for them. Well, no use thinking about that any more. The grown-ups had made their decisions and that was all there was to it. She sighed, and accepted the plate Annie passed to her. Jackie living at the van, Teddy Hooson likely to be gone from Beckindale in a week or so . . . She felt she'd be swamped in this houseful of older people.

The conversation at the tea-table was dominated by Dolly, bubbling with happiness over her new prospects. As soon as the meal was over she dragged Matt out with her, to survey her new home.

'Eh, lad,' she murmured as they stood inside the barn door, arms around each other. 'I'm glad we're not going, aren't you?'

'Aye, glad . . . and relieved . . . and yet . . .'

'What, love? You're pleased, aren't you?'

'Of course I am. But do you think we're being selfish, taking this away from Pat and Jack?'

'Oh, Matt!' She dragged him close and kissed him vehemently. 'Only you would bother about a thing like that!'

'All t'same, Dolly –'

'I'm not going to think about that! It was our place, we thought of it first and we deserved it – at least you did. And the fact that we've got it means they see – Jack sees – who's really important around here.'

'Nay, Dolly, that's no way to talk.'

'It's the truth. And I'm not the only one who knows a

good man when I see one!'

Matt laughed. 'Don't go making me big-headed! Come on, love, let's have that tape-measure. Let's mark out the size of the kitchen.'

She took the tape-measure out of her pocket and gave it to him. As he moved about the interior, murmuring measurements to himself, she leaned in the doorway and looked out towards the sunlight over the evening fields.

She had never wanted to leave Emmerdale. She knew that Matt had never wanted to either. For once, things had worked out right for Matt.

Perhaps that was all that was wanted – a little pugnacity, a little determination. She must remember to try it again, next time it was needed.